Praise For Night Lights

Here in the Northwest, we recognize our good fortune in having a community of talented writers. Now, in this representative collection, fans of good writing near and far can share our pleasure as they read these short stories and essays by a wildly diverse group of authors. Some are humorous, some startling serious, and all are entertaining. We're fortunate indeed to have Humanities Washington's annual Bedtime Stories event to inspire this creativity and new work.

> — Nancy Pearl
> Author of *Book Lust: Recommended Reading for Every Mood, Moment, and Reason*

In *Night Lights*, 21 Pacific Northwest authors prove that rain and coffee and the salt of sea air do indeed enhance the creative process. Their unique stories serve up a little poetry, a dash of tall story, and a penchant for saying what is most true, resulting in this engaging collection. It is a welcome addition to any Northwest literature enthusiast's library.

> — Jennie Shortridge
> Author of *When She Flew* and other novels

Humanities Washington's Bedtime Stories event is the one event writers consider the literary event *for writers*. Once each year a mere 200 people are invited to hear beautiful original stories read aloud for the first time. With the publication of this anthology, everyone is invited to the party now.

> — Shawn Wong
> Author of *Homebase* and *American Knees*

This collection suggests that artists find fertile ground when inspired by inventive themes. It dispels the notion that art must be spontaneous, and in this collection, we reap the fruit.

> — David Guterson
> Author of *The Other* and *Snow Falling on Cedars*

ISBN: 145360894X
ISBN-13: 9781453608944

NIGHT*lights*

Stories & Essays
from 21 Northwest Authors

Foreword by Dr. Charles Johnson

CREDITS AND COPYRIGHTS

PUBLISHER'S NOTE
OF THANKS

This book is dedicated to our extraordinary
Bedtime Stories authors whose talent and
generosity have helped raise more than
$500,000 for Humanities Washington's
statewide cultural and education programs.

All proceeds from the sales of *Night Lights* will
support Humanities Washington's work to promote
inquiry, insight, and inspiration
in communities across the state.

ABOUT HUMANITIES WASHINGTON

Since 1973, Humanities Washington has served nearly half a million people annually through programs that touch every corner of Washington State—from Aberdeen to Zillah, Seattle to Spokane—connecting Washingtonians from all backgrounds and communities by honoring and sharing stories, ideas, and perspectives, and enabling us to understand our past and present as we work to shape our future.

Through reading, writing, storytelling, conversation, presentations, and other avenues, Humanities Washington reaches out to all to advance thoughtful and engaged communities by creating a deeper understanding of who we are and the remarkable, challenging, and inspiring experiences that connect us.

The humanities – including history, literature, philosophy, ethics, law and other fields of inquiry—provide valuable opportunities to learn more about our personal perspectives; test and challenge our ideas and biases; and explore a range of positions including the gray area between polarizing opinions.

The humanities reflect our past, but just as importantly, our present and future, serving as a dynamic light to engage, inspire, challenge, and empower Washingtonians by encouraging us to investigate, speak, listen, read, reflect, question, think, grow, and act.

For more information on our programs and work across the state, visit www.humanities.org.

TABLE OF CONTENTS

FOREWORD

Bedtime Stories, the most exciting literary experience every year in Seattle, began quietly in 1999 when Margaret Ann Bollmeier, then Humanities Washington's executive director, asked me to serve on the board of that organization. With that membership, there came a duty—people on the board served on different committees, and so I needed to select one. As it turned out, the board was thinking about having local authors read their fiction at a fund-raising event that would help Humanities Washington's outstanding cultural and education programs; for example, Motheread/Fatheread, a program focused on building literacy skills of parents so they may read to their children and harness the power of language to discover more about themselves, their families, and their communities.

Now, I have nothing against authors reading their published work, which at the time was something I'd done for twenty-seven years; and since the late 1960s, I'd been to literally hundreds of poetry and fiction readings like the one board members were naturally thinking about. The format was commonplace. But I confessed to Margaret Ann how weary I was, personally, of reading my own stories written years ago. Try to imagine what it's like for me to read today a chapter from *Middle Passage*, which was published in 1990. It may be fresh for a new generation of listeners, but for this author twenty years later, it's a work I've progressed far beyond in my life. Where, I wondered, was the artistic *challenge* in reading old material? Furthermore, I said, the writers who I hold in highest esteem are, first and foremost, *storytellers*. I've always envisioned my ideal writer to be a raconteur with a robust imagination, a man or woman capable of conjuring on demand a spirited entertainment on *any* subject he or she is asked to dramatize. "Can we do something like that?" I asked. "Have all the participants this year create a new story?" And Margaret Ann, bless her, said okay.

That first year the theme was simply "Bedtime Stories." And what a happy choice that was, for in every child's life, during those early years of innocence and trust, the magical story filled with mystery and wonder told at the end of the day— by parents or perhaps grand-parents—to help us sleep and seed our dreams pre-dates all the other kinds of stories we experience in life. Or think of this in terms of our ancestors spinning tales around a campfire, their voices holding the other members of the tribe enthralled for hours on end, there in the darkness where the story and its characters—and the question "What happens next?"—were as brightly lit in their minds as the embers of the campfire itself.

And so a tradition began. Every year since 1999, the board has selected a topic—always a surprise for the writers who participate—related to the nocturnal. Some years they have caused this writer to dive deep into the well of my imagination, finding depths I never knew were there. For these themes have been nothing if not diverse from year to year.

As daunting an enterprise as it has been every year to create a new story for a wide-ranging list of topics, I must say that this rare opportunity to do so has been a creative blessing for me, demanding but also deeply rewarding (and full of self-discovery) as few assignments have been in my forty-five years of publishing fiction. Over the span of a decade, the Bedtime Stories event has nudged me to create an expansive range of short fictions that I simply would never have dreamed of doing on my own. Never! Furthermore, all the stories I've written for this event have been published, several of them reprinted and anthologized often, broadcast on radio station KUOW in Seattle, and one ("A Kiss Goodnight," which I renamed "Cultural Relativity") was made into a short film by David S. DeCrane and shown at the Newport Beach Film Festival on April 17, 2004. Five of the stories are in my third story collection, *Dr. King's Refrigerator and Other Bedtime Stories* (the title story sprang from the topic "midnight snack"), and four appear in the philosophy textbook I co-authored this year with Michael Boylan, *Philosophy, An Innovative Introduction: Fictive Narrative, Primary Texts, and Responsive Writing.*

My friend the late playwright August Wilson also greatly enjoyed creating fiction for Bedtime Stories when his always-demanding schedule allowed him to be in Seattle during the fall. Like medieval troubadours, we both relished the chance to test anew our storytelling prowess and see what the other had managed to come up with. During our conversations before the event (we receive our theme from the board in spring and have until October to get the story done), August would ask me (or vice versa), "You got *yours* done yet?" and in this playfully asked question there was always a poke of the elbow to one's ribs, a gauntlet thrown down, a twinge of the competitive delight that two veteran artists experience when they are handed the exact same problem to solve (or two kids daring each other to do something), and the immense satisfaction they have when the other stands at the microphone and delivers a job well done (which the rest of the world will only learn about later)—but not for money. Or even publication. No, all the writers have created their Bedtime Stories for free, and in the spirit of generosity that jazz musicians enjoy when they sit down for an after-hours jam session, trading off riffs on a single musical theme ("Yeah," one might say, "That was good, but can you top *this?*"), and learning from each other during a festive evening of good food, good fellowship, and good fiction.

Thanks to Humanities Washington, those are the kind of stories you hold in your hands, entertainments that sprang from the purest creative impulse, from the pleasure skillful literary artists enjoy when they are given the chance to just do their thing—like world-class athletes relaxed and at play, performing not for a gold trophy but simply because exercising their hard-won skills feels so danged good.

If you enjoy rousing, good storytelling, and aesthetic diversity in fiction, then this volume offers inexhaustible treasures.

Dr. Charles Johnson
Seattle, 2010

BEDTIME STORIES THEMES
1999-2009

Photo Courtesy of Alexa Robbins.

Tom Robbins has published nine offbeat but popular novels in 22 languages. His numerous essays and stories, collected in *Wild Ducks Flying Backward* in 2005, have appeared in periodicals ranging from *Playboy* to *Harpers*, *Esquire* to the *New York Times*. An honors graduate of Virginia Commonwealth University, he has divided his time between Seattle and La Conner, Washington since 1962.

Tom read his story, *Teriyaki Astronaut*, at the 2004 Bedtime Stories event themed "Dreamland."

TERIYAKI ASTRONAUT

Once upon a time (and all the best bedtime stories begin this way), toward the end of the Second World War, an American bomber, damaged by anti-aircraft fire, crashed in the rugged mountains of north central Japan. An investigating party from a remote mountain village made its way to the crash site, where it discovered that the pilot of the demolished plane was miraculously alive. The badly injured flyer was extricated from the wreckage and carried back to the village.

Now, the villagers, devout Buddhists one and all, possessed the Buddhistic reverence for all life without exception. They were, moreover, physically and psychologically far removed from the hot arena of geopolitical events and the ugly ambitions that had set those events in motion. It's not surprising, therefore, that they elected to take in the American pilot and secretly nurse him. Ignoring the considerable risks involved, they kept him concealed and alive for several months, although eventually, to their sorrow, he died.

Hand in hand with a reverence for life goes a respect for the proprieties, the protocol, of death. The universe—the *dharma* if you will—demands it. So the villagers felt it incumbent upon them to give the pilot a proper burial. Alas, the only funereal practices with which they were familiar were Buddhistic, and those, of course, would have been inappropriate. Perplexed, they packed the corpse in pond ice and pondered the situation.

As time went by, they set out to make inquiries about Christian burial traditions (it never occurred to anyone to check for absence of foreskin), all very discreetly so as not to arouse the suspicion of authorities. Their luck was small.

Then they had another idea. It seems there was a bright young woman in the hamlet who, just before the war, had worked as a maid at the U.S. consulate in Kyoto, where she had picked up a fair amount of English. They dispatched the ex-maid to Kyoto, on foot, to visit the great library there to see what she might learn about Western rites of lamentation and internment.

Browsing, as inconspicuously as possible, through the sparse English language section of the Kyoto public library, the woman suddenly came upon a volume that promised to be the perfect guidebook to the rites her community felt compelled to perform. Emboldened by this stroke of luck, she hid the book inside her kimono and smuggled it out of the building.

The book was called *Finnegans Wake*.

Well, if any of you have ever attempted to read James Joyce's famous novel—and only about a dozen people on the entire planet have actually succeeded in reading it cover to cover—you know that *Finnegans Wake* is 628 pages of what is unarguably the most linguistically dense and challenging prose ever composed by a writer of fiction, a maddening stream-of-consciousness non-linear masterpiece written almost completely in a code of Joyce's own devising, resplendent with wordplay, onomatopoeia, and non-stop punning; puns layered on top of puns like ingredients on a submarine sandwich, puns not only in English and Celtic but Latin, Greek, Abyssinian, and Sanskrit; puns that refer obliquely to the more obscure particulars of Irish politics, world history, mythology, archaeology, music, art, pornography, and medical science. In short, less a novel in any conventional sense than a gigantic psychedelic crossword puzzle, twitching with erudite tomfoolery and pumped up on intellectual steroids.

So—imagine if you can those isolated, simple, uneducated Japanese yam farmers earnestly trying to organize a funeral using *Finnegans Wake* as a blueprint.

Yet, try they did. And—they're still trying. Burial services for the downed American pilot began in 1945—and now, six decades later, are still going on: week after week, year after year, Molly Bloomsday after Molly Bloomsday, and with little sign of stopping since, at last report, the mourners were only up to page 34 in the book.

The most notable change in the proceedings occurred in the late 1960s, when the peasants took up a collection and purchased a portable electrical generator. As a result, the pilot's cadaver now lies at rest in an Amana freezer. I know because I've stared at it (a freezer stare, by the way, very, very different from trying to decide which item you're going to thaw out for dinner).

Having learned about these bizarre goings on from a drunken stranger in a Tokyo sake bar—and, fascinated though incredulous—I made a pilgrimage to the village last December and spent a day there, masquerading as an Amana repairman on a courtesy service call. I'm here to report that it was literally like entering dreamland: a sustained, expansive, three-dimensional, around-the-clock, wakeful communal dream.

All activity in the village is fragmented. A constant dislocation of temporal and spatial perspective defies ordinary reality, leaving the inhabitants free from the dictates of common sense, including, for example, the logic of walking upright or eating with the hands instead of the feet. People there seldom display any distinct evidence of individual personality, but rather exist as composites and amalgamations (just as in your own dream, two ex-lovers might appear combined in a single figure, with, say, a bit of Ozzie Osborne or Lindsay Lohan thrown in for good measure); and most disconcertedly, the speech of the villagers is subject to frequent surprising outbursts of scholarly Norwegian, alchemical equations, arcane medical references, witty puns, double entendre, and enough pure Irish blarney to overwhelm every pub in Glockamara.

Unfortunately, I cannot be more specific. As you are well aware, dreams are difficult to remember. Unlike the occurrences in our wakeful lives, dreams, for some reason, fail to imprint the electrochemical cells in our memory banks: a dream will move uninvited into your cerebral penthouse, rearrange the furniture, paint over the wallpaper, throw a wild party, set the cat on fire, then depart abruptly without paying the phone bill or leaving a forwarding address. Similarly, within hours after snowboarding out of that possessed village in my rented Nissan Pathfinder, I'd forgotten virtually every detail that I observed there.

There has been, however, some residue. Have you ever, as you went about your daily life, been visited unexpectedly by a spark, a crumb, a stray fragment from a forgotten dream of the night before? As often as not, these brief flashes of recollection are verbal. You'll suddenly recall a line that was spoken in the dream— and the words will seem *significant* somehow, if only you could place them in context, could remember exactly to what they'd referred. There's a message there, you think, some potentially useful insight, perhaps even a precious diamond of life-altering wisdom—but it's frustratingly evasive, you can't quite put your finger on it.

In recent months, I've experienced out of nowhere two such illuminations, two vague epiphanies that I honestly believe to be subliminal echoes of words I heard spoken in that curious mountain village in rural Japan. For what it's worth, I'd like to share the messages with you and let *you* be the judge of their profundity.

Message #1: "Should you, in your personal evolution, in your long and persistent search for meaning in life, finally pierce the veils of illusion, rip away the mask of consensual reality, come face to face with ultimate truth, and see clearly how the universe works and how it all adds up, you will thereupon find yourself shaking your head and saying over and over again, 'This is absolutely nothing like I thought it would be.'"

Message #2: "Only the survivors are lost."

Photo Copyright © Libby Lewis.

Margot Kahn published her first book, *Horses That Buck*, in 2008. She is the recipient of a Hertog Fellowship from Columbia University (2003), the Ohioana Library Association's Walter Marvin Rumsey Award for a promising writer under 30 (2005), the High Plains "Best First Book" Award (2009), a CityArtist Award from the City of Seattle Office of Arts & Cultural Affairs (2010) and an Individual Artist Award from 4Culture (2010). She holds an MFA in creative writing from Columbia University and has worked professionally as a journalist, speechwriter and arts administrator. She currently curates creative writing programs for teens at Richard Hugo House in Seattle, Washington, and is working on a collection of essays.

Margot read her story, *Dream House*, at the 2009 event themed "In Your Dreams."

DREAM HOUSE

When my husband and I had been married for not quite five weeks, we fell in love with a house—a 1923 Craftsman with original oak floors and divided light windows in every room. A magical garden of Japanese maples, rhododendrons, ferns and black bamboo presided in front, and a slender, private deck beckoned in back. We surveyed the bathroom counter constructed of broken Fiestaware plates set haphazardly in grout; the octopus furnace holding in its arms and body all of its charming, original asbestos; the seven stone temples, Buddha shrine and two small mosquito-infested ponds in the front yard. It was 2005, and we had already lost one house to a bidding war with six other prospective buyers. With this one, I thought, "We have a chance." And I was right. We bid under asking, and two weeks later, we owned the place—Buddha, water features, asbestos and all.

Before we set out to hire a contractor, my husband and I agreed that we had to agree: we both had to fall in love all over again. We would be working intimately with whomever we hired to create the space we were going to call home, and we wanted someone who would know how to listen, someone who would care. The first guy we called showed up in a shiny, black F350. He had his cell phone clipped to his belt, and it rang twice before he answered it. I didn't like the way he spoke to the woman on the other end, and my husband didn't like the size of his truck. The second contender was a soccer player, which won over my husband instantly, but the guy never looked me in the eye. The third one made it clear that our project was too small for him. The fourth was insanely shy. And then John arrived.

John had been curt on the phone, somewhat hard of hearing, and he couldn't meet us until the end of the week because, he told me, he was having a colonoscopy. But on Friday he arrived in a respectably beat-up, blank, white van, and he wore respectably used but tidy, clean, ironed coveralls. His hair was the color of sea salt. A hearing aid was tucked behind his left ear, and his back curved in two directions: in a smooth round across the shoulder blades, and softly—like a fern—along the spine. He carried a paper cup of coffee through our empty rooms and looked around quietly, touching nothing. We told him what we were thinking: Take the bathroom and the kitchen down to the studs; rebuild the master bedroom cabinetry; re-wire and re-plumb; refinish the floors.

John nodded and explained that he had a few retired friends he called out to help him on jobs like this—a retired electrician and a retired plumber and a friend from the VFW who didn't mind painting—but that he would do all the other work himself and would be there every day until the job was done. For me, it was like the time my husband wrote on a tablecloth at a fancy restaurant in New York City "kiss, please" upside-down so I could read it, and I knew right then, on our second date, that I would marry him. As soon as John left the house, I said, "I love him!" And my husband said, "I love him, too."

The very next week, John was at work on our house. His equipment was surprisingly rickety—a wooden ladder that looked like it had been rescued from a shipwreck and old-school sheetrock stilts that I was truly afraid for him to wear. He dressed in Dickies and kept a knife-sharpened pencil in his pocket or behind his ear. From a paint-smudged boom box, he blasted 98.1 KING FM. Accompanied by plaster falling, a table-saw spinning, a hammer driving nails into thick, hard, wood, John and his symphonies gave our house a feeling of impeccable, elated, muscular elegance.

One day in the drenched dark of winter, John called me at my office. "The dining room floor there where it meets the north wall —" he said, "it's sagging by three quarters of an inch. I jacked up the house and propped a 6x6 under the stairs, but you might want to come by tonight while I'm here and have a look." When I got off the phone my co-worker said, "You were *cooing*."

"My 70-year-old contractor just *jacked up my house*," I tried to explain. But I couldn't replicate his old voice that sounded like sand inside the rhinoceros's skin. This was a gritty man, a man who could handle anything, who was surprised by nothing. And I, knowing nothing about jacks, studs, or plumbing stacks, was glad to be completely in his hands. When I called my husband and told him the story, he was equally impressed, conjuring the same image I had, of John alone in the cool basement setting his hands up against the exposed beams and lifting our entire house with the flats of his palms. Later that evening, as we stood in the basement looking at the concrete feet he'd poured to replace the rotted old posts, John said he had tried what he thought would work, but the post had sunk back into the earth just as soon as he'd removed the jack. I asked him if it was something we should be concerned about, the house sinking, the floor sagging, the walls cracking.

"Well, it's been here 85 years," he said. And that was all.

On spare weekends, my husband and I took on small jobs to help the project along. As the months wore on and our house was torn apart, we saw her insides: the way the lath lay imperfectly parallel, the way the wires nestled themselves between the studs. At night, the basement lights would shine up through holes in the sub-floor like stars. One day, when we came home from work, John handed me the recipes he'd found inside the kitchen's east wall. On a coupon for flour, the back of which shared instructions for "Everyday Cake," someone had penciled in the expiration, 1/3/43. I wanted to kiss him in the dent between his cheekbone and his coarse, white beard.

When the project was done, two months late and a little over budget, my husband and I said goodbye to John. In the years since, there have been countless trips to Home Depot, standard maintenance and regular repairs. Rats have been in the attic, robins have nested on the porch, and paper wasps have commandeered the branches above our front gate. Last year, someone punched a hole in the glass kitchen door, let themselves in and took all the electronic stuff. The back deck turned out to be rotten, and we pulled it up and put in a garden. Whenever we have a heavy rain, a rivulet runs from west to east across the basement's thin concrete floor. When that happens, I think of John. I stand where the floor is sagging, in the very center of the house, where the dining room meets the north wall, and it feels as steady as can be. I stand there because the curve of the floor feels good beneath my feet, and because it reminds me that home is built of solid but imperfect things: window glass and table salt, constant work and dreams of what is yet to come.

Photo Copyright © Sean McDowell.

Samuel Green is the author of ten poetry collections, including *The Grace of Necessity*, which recently won the Washington State Book Award for Poetry. For nearly 30 years he has served as co-publisher, with his wife, Sally, of Brooding Heron Press. Sam has been a Distinguished Visiting Northwest Writer at Seattle University for a decade, and is active with the Skagit River Poetry Festival. In 2008 he was named to a two-year post as the first Poet Laureate of the State of Washington. In 2009, Sam was awarded a National Endowment for the Arts Fellowship in Poetry.

Sam read his story, *Into the Territory*, at the 2009 event themed "In Your Dreams."

INTO THE TERRITORY

Our son's bedroom resembles a giant kitchen table with six-foot legs. Sally and I are short, so we walk beneath it with ease. Visitors need to bend. Really, it's only two sheets of plywood tacked onto a frame, with four-by-fours for legs and a wooden ladder nailed to one side. Lonnie is eight, and he scampers up the rungs like a chipmunk to a foam pad nest surrounded by toys and baskets of clothes.

The bedroom fills the middle section of the surplus army tent in which we now live. Under his floor are book shelves, and the futon his mother and I roll out each night. The main floor is also made of plywood: twelve sheets squared on a frame set on top of a series of cedar logs dragged from the woods. Each evening, after the futon is made up for bed, Lonnie sprawls across it, loose-limbed, listening to me read from *Huckleberry Finn*. I sit in a rocking chair fashioned from tree limbs, leaning toward the warm, yellow light of a kerosene lamp, book held open in my left hand. Sally rocks in a second chair near another lamp, darning socks, sewing patches on the knees of dungarees, crocheting. Her small hands seem always to be full of one sort of work or another, like small birds that can't stay still. Occasionally she rises to tend the fire in our kitchen range, a Round Oak made in the 'twenties, or to stir a pot of goat stew simmering on a trivet farthest away from the fire box. At the other end of the tent, there's a barrel stove I made from a kit. The two fires make enough heat to bully the late October chill into the farthest corners. The good smell of wood smoke never entirely leaves.

It is 1982. Only a few months ago we lived in a comfortable cinder block home in north Seattle, commuting to jobs in the city while our son lingered in daycare and school. It wasn't what we wanted. We dreamed of a life that would keep us together full time, allow us to write poems, make books, learn what it meant to own ourselves. So we sold our house and everything electric, and moved onto ten acres of logged-over land in the middle of a tiny island, about a hundred miles north. It's an island without many conveniences: no sewer system, no public water, no electricity, no telephones, no stores. A post office offers mail three days a week (if the weather is good), and a tiny school a mile away serves the first eight grades. The only way on or off is by private boat or air taxi. We are roughly in the center. Two miles in any direction, and we wade into cold water. Though we can't know it, we will live in the tent for three years, while I build a log house.

We have no television, and can't yet afford batteries for a radio, let alone a radio itself. Instead, there are books. We've already read *Tom Sawyer* out loud. In the year to come, we'll read the whole *Swallows & Amazons* series, *The Hobbit*, *The Lord of the Rings*. Lonnie never gets tired of listening. He stretches out on his stomach across the futon, chin resting in the heels of his palms, watching the way my lips move, the gestures of my right hand, how my body shifts back and forth in the rocker. Or he lies on his side, one ear turned to the tight, green canvas roof, letting words fall into his ears like nickels pitched into cups at a carnival. We read for an hour or two every night. When we get to a stopping place, he is filled with dismay: *Just one more page, please, please, pretty-pretty please!* It will be this impatience that will finally push him into reading for himself. Some kids become so hungry for story they will jump into the roughest current of language and flail bravely until they learn how to stay afloat, the way Lonnie and his classmates have learned to roll over kayaks and canoes in one of the small ponds, so they can go safely on field trips to other islands.

Living as we do, it isn't hard to imagine Huck and Jim on the raft, floating lazily under a southern sun, fishing lines dangled over the side. When he takes his pole to the county dock, Lonnie keeps one flap on his overalls loose, the way he imagines Huck might, and goes barefoot until the cold finally chases him into shoes.

In our first months, both Lonnie and Sally sleep soundly, but I lie awake, listening through the thin membrane of canvas: raindrops falling on the waxy leaves of Oregon grape; rats rummaging through branches of ocean spray; the occasional scream of a rabbit dying in a rush of feathers and fur. We can follow a low flock of geese for miles. If a neighbor is up late, driving on the narrow gravel roads, we know whose car it is by the sound of the engine. There are few secrets in this small place. Sometimes Lonnie tries to postpone bedtime by asking for one of the poems my father taught me. *Do it with a voice, Dad.*

And we'll have Peter Lorre doing "The Shooting of Dan McGrew":

> "A bunch of the boys were whooping it up, in the Malamute Saloon."

Or James Mason intoning "The Cremation of Sam McGee":

> "Now Sam McGee was from Tennessee, where the cotton blooms and blows."

I know these old poems by heart, and it isn't long before my son begins mouthing the words with me, grinning like an otter at his favorite lines.

When fall storms begin, like elephants lined up trunk to tail offshore, waiting for their turn in the ring, I get up several times a night with a flashlight and search for leaks, or for some sign the tent is about to collapse around us. But when the strongest gusts come bucking down the shoulder of the mountain, like a logging truck without brakes, the tent walls simply push in and out, gently. It's like living in a giant lung. Even on still nights I am unsettled, so I get up, untie the tent flaps and step outside to see frost clamped to the ground, the moon like a brooch on a black shawl, Orion stalking the sky above the clearing. It's hard to believe we haven't made a mistake, that we aren't going to have to pay a hard price for happiness.

Each morning we ask Lonnie how he slept. *Fine*, he says. *Did you dream?* He tells us:

> I was a barnacle that got tired of its rock.
> *What did you do?*
> Let go, and went to find another.
> *Were you afraid?*
> No.
> *Were you sad to leave your friends?*
> There are lots of barnacles. I was just looking for a rock that wanted me.

His imagination can be risky. When we were building our tent platform, we slept on an old logging road. Lonnie complained of the "ripply" ground beneath his sleeping bag. I told him those were caterpillar tracks. He spent the long night with visions of hairy giants wriggling through our camp to crush us all. Another time

I woke to find he'd joined us on the futon, his head pressed to Sally's chest. When he saw me watching, he whispered: *I was afraid her heart might stop. You know, the way the frogs quit singing, sometimes.* It takes months to realize most of his dreams have to do with life-change, and risk.

The ritual of reading helps him think in terms of narrative. Each day, when he comes bursting through the tent flap, he tells how many seals he saw near the dock, how many white-headed eagles perched on the dead limbs of snags above the beach. Like Twain, he's a good observer, and has a heart as open as the eyes of an owl.

Tom's elaborate plans to rescue Jim from the shed make perfect sense to Lonnie. It doesn't occur to him that we haul water because we don't yet have the money to drill our own well; in his mind, pulling a garden cart full of buckets nearly a mile from a neighbor's well simply makes a better yarn, draws it out, adds flavor. He *likes* drinking from the tin dipper that hangs above the bucket just outside the back door.

He tells spontaneous stories of his own:

> Was a whale, wanted to turn into a big, floating tree.
> *Why?*
> So birds would have some place to land when they got tired.

When I imitate him, he gets impatient:

> *Was a boy who wanted to be a bear.*
> *No!* Was a *bear*, who wanted to be a *boy.*

We begin to add our own adventures to island lore: an otter steals a bag of fish after we leave it on the steps of the post office for only a few minutes; a tiny screech owl gets into our chicken coop and kills a chick, but then clings, terrified, to the wire screen as the broody hen charges back and forth in a hurricane of feathers. We have to rescue it. I think of Robert Frost a good deal in these days, his lines about the land being ours before we were the land's.

We come to the famous end of Huck Finn: "I reckon I got to light out for the territory ahead of the rest, because Aunt Sally, she's going to adopt me, civilize me, and I can't stand it. I've been there before."

I hate to close the book. It stays open on my lap. Lonnie is silent for a time, then asks, *Are we in the territory?* His question startles us. Of course we are. Why haven't we noticed? We, too, have slid off the current of the river in order to avoid someone else's idea of how we are supposed to live, and headed off to stake a claim in the wild territory of ourselves. Now we're proving it up.

I ask if he wishes he knew what happened to Huck, afterward.

> *Why?*
> So we'd know what to do.
> *Dad, we're writing our* own *story!*

And so we are. Like birds that fly through the sound of their own calling, we hadn't realized it. A few days later Lonnie asks what *I* dream about. I tell him I don't remember dreams very often, and that maybe I don't dream at all. He laughs.

> You're dreaming right now.
> *What?*
> I remember, before we moved, you told somebody we were gonna be living our dream.

He's right again. Twain says that in dreams, "we do make the journeys we seem to make: we do see the things we seem to see; the people, the homes, the cats, the dogs, the birds, the whales, are real . . ." We have given ourselves over to what dreams and story have made possible, their attentive care, their eloquent keeping.

Photo by Jerry Bauer.

Kathleen Alcalá is the author of five books whose trilogy on nineteenth century Mexico was published by Chronicle Books. Her work has received the Western States Book Award, the Governor's Writers Award, a Pacific Northwest Bookseller's Award, and a Washington State Book Award. A co-founder and contributing editor to *The Raven Chronicles*, Kathleen teaches at the Northwest Institute of Literary Arts on Whidbey Island, a low-residency program. She was recently deemed an Island Treasure by the Bainbridge Island Arts and Humanities Council, and has work in the new *Norton Anthology of Latino Literature*.

Kathleen read her story, *The Light on the Midway*, at the 2007 event themed "Night Light."

THE LIGHT ON THE MIDWAY

At the age of thirteen, I walked the length of the midway at the National Orange Show. Renamed in 1911 by the San Bernardino citrus growers to advertise their product, this was our county fair. Dusk was coming on, and the day people, with their sunburns and tired, whining, sticky-handed children, were leaving. The agricultural exhibits inside the Swing Auditorium began to close—glistening pyramids of oranges, ears of sweet corn, and award-winning home-baked pies. The Future Farmers of America began to take home the baby animals that had blue ribbons pinned to their enclosures. The rhythm of the fair changed as the light began to fail, and my pulse quickened with it.

One by one, or in small groups, the night people replaced them— teenagers with long, bleached hair in absurdly wide bell bottoms, couples who had worked all day, single men. I walked the midway once, then again, until a carny called out to me from one of the booths, "What you lookin' for, darlin'?" I felt myself blush and quickly walked away. I think I shook my head at him, unable even to begin to say what it was.

That summer, I listened to the police scanner late at night on a combination radio walky-talky my uncle had given me. Interested in electronics himself, he often gave his nieces and nephews clocks and weather gauges, radios and watches. We were not sure where he got these things, probably at an electronic outlet store, since at the time, many of them were specialty items. I was thrilled with the radio walkie-talkie—it opened up the wide world of the night sky, the clear channel stations, and the weird, wacky and wonderful things that people talked about. It was an entire universe of insomniacs preoccupied with obscure music, outrageous crimes, and UFOs.

That was when the night really caught my imagination. Especially in a desert climate, people's behavior changed late at night. My parents thought only indecent people went out after dark, people up to no good, so of course I yearned to know what those people might do. I stayed up late reading and "day" dreaming, wondering about where people travelled, what they wore, what set a "decent" person apart from an indecent person.

Our house stood at the busy intersection of Sixteenth and "H" streets. Across "H" street was an apartment house. It had probably been built in the forties, just prior to most of the houses in the neighborhood, with a courtyard at the center that was open to the street, and the single-story apartments set around the three sides. It had big trees, and generally did not call attention to itself. Most of the people who lived there did not stay very long, and with one or two exceptions, we did not get to know them. This is the same apartment house mentioned by Ricardo Pimentel in his novel, *The House with Two Doors*, set during the Viet Nam era. In the novel, the narrator's father moves there after his parents break up over the father's infidelity.

As the weather heated up, so did the activity at the apartment house. On the weekends there were many comings and goings, lots of car traffic, but generally, it was quiet, especially during the day. One weekend, however, someone must have called the police.

I was drifting on the edge of sleep when I heard an address near ours mentioned on the police scanner, so I stood up, put on my glasses, and looked out of my second story window. By now, both of my sisters were living elsewhere, so I was alone upstairs. Sure enough, police cars began to pull up a block away, and officers got out of the cars and began to creep up stealthily on the apartments. I had a clear view of the whole scene.

Soon there was pounding on doors, and shouting and screaming. People began to bolt from the rooms half-dressed, only to land in the arms of the police. One couple made it into the thick bushes on the south side of the apartments, and stayed there. The woman looked up and spotted me, then pressed her finger to her lips, entreating me to not give them away. I cannot remember if the police brought a paddy wagon, but soon most of the residents and visitors had been carted off. It was a beautiful night for a raid, warm and clear.

When the police had finished mopping up, I gave the "all clear" signal to the couple, who came out of the plants. I could see that they were very pleased not to have been arrested, and I imagine now that in some ways, they had a better adventure than if they had stayed in the dreary apartment.

Shortly after that, the apartments were under new management and had new residents. I don't think I ever spoke to the woman who saw me. She could not exactly come over and say thank you.

When I think back on the apartment house raid, the night sky is backlit to the west with the lights from the freeway and the railroad yards. All the lights are on in the individual apartments, glowing yellow in the deepening night. The man and woman hiding outside are well-dressed—she in a fashionable dress, he in a suit. Their clothing is vaguely forties-style. They are smiling. They are having fun. It is lit like an Edward Hopper painting, and I am transported by the beauty of the scene. I doubt that I am remembering this accurately, but indulge me.

After all the police cars finally pulled away, there was an emptiness that made me sad. In all the excitement, I had forgotten what was really going on: people were going to jail.

That was the year I had been at the county fair by myself. I don't know how I managed that, or if I was temporarily separated from a group of friends. The night smelled like fried foods, like marijuana smoke, like danger, like things that could happen if one was not a decent person. When the carny called out, "What you lookin' for, darlin'?" I felt as though I had been caught out, as though he had seen something in me that I was forbidden to think or feel.

That question has haunted me ever since. I did not know what I was looking for. I only knew that I was filled with a deep yearning for something outside of my limited experience. As the years unfolded, I would find some of these things. I would read a book and walk, as if in a daze, with the volume pressed to my chest out of sheer gratitude. I would sit by the radio and sob at the wrenching sound of a solo cello. And yes, I would lose myself in the bliss of another person's body.

Not all of the things I yearned for were profoundly transcendent. I haggled for a reproduction of a print by Matisse in New York City and for years decorated my homes with it. Years later, in a restaurant in Williams, California, an older Japanese American made origami for my son, who gave him drawings in exchange. Recently, a bookseller on Capitol Hill extolled the virtues of a homeless kitten she was trying to give away. A friend who was with me said, "Wherever you go, people tell you stories." With the passing years,

I find that I still love this world and many of its imperfections. An athlete was recently quoted in *The Seattle Times*, saying the opposite of what I have always been taught. Kit DesLauriers, who has skied off the highest peak on each of the world's seven continents, said "we are really spiritual people trying to live a physical existence."

We think our inner lives are secret, ultimately unknowable. In that respect, we are all alike. We recognize the light in Edward Hopper's paintings because it is asking the question, "What you looking for, darlin'?" It is the late-night light of the insomniac, the nonconformist, the artist. Even when together, his characters are alone, refusing to make eye contact with each other. I can easily imagine myself as the woman leaning towards the window in "Eleven a.m." or stepping out the door in "Cape Cod Morning," her lover behind her, each ignoring the other.

Or perhaps his work gives the only possible answer.

"If you could say it in words," said Hopper, "there would be no reason to paint."

"Hopper's is an art of illuminated outsides," according to Peter Schjeldahl in *The New Yorker*, "that bespeak important insides. He vivifies impenetrable privacies. Notice how seldom he gives houses visible or, if visible, usable-looking doors; but the windows are alive. His preoccupied people will neither confirm nor deny any fantasy they stir; their intensity of being defeats conjecture. Imputations, to them, of 'loneliness' are sentimental projections by viewers who ought to look harder. They may not have lives you envy, but they live them without complaint."

The girl on the midway was alone, but not lonely. The man and woman evading the police raid were looking for something together, but probably not the same thing. Listening to the radio late on summer nights, we feel our separateness, we relate to the disembodied voices. But by the light on the midway, the backlighting of the police raid, and the light in Edward Hopper's paintings, we are reminded that light, that most intangible of observable events, is physical, and that physicality, our greatest weakness, is beautiful.

Photo Copyright © Tananarive Due.

Steven Barnes is a lecturer, coach, novelist and television writer and has published about two million words of science fiction (including the *New York Times* bestsellers *The Legacy of Heorot* and *The Cestus Deception*) written twenty hours of produced television shows (including *The Twilight Zone, Outer Limits, Andromeda,* and *Stargate,* as well as four episodes of the immortal *Baywatch*). Barnes lives in California with his wife, Tananarive Due. For more information on his work visit stevenbarnesblog.com.

At the 2001 event (themed "A Kiss Goodnight"), Steve read a chapter from the novel *Lion's Blood* (Warner Books, 2002). The story of an alternate 1880 "America" (here called "Bilalistan") colonized by Islamic Africans, it follows two protagonists: Irish slave Aidan O'Dere and Kai ibn Jallaleddin ibn Rashid, heir to the most powerful estate in all New Djibouti (Texas). In this excerpt, Kai and his brother's fiancée Lamiya have been kidnapped by runaway slaves and face an uncertain future…

CHAPTER FIFTY-SEVEN

If not for the circumstances, Kai might have found the journey downstream almost peaceful. Frogs sang to them as they floated, and the wings of night insects beat feverishly among the fronds. A salt wind blew from the south, stirring the trees and whispering of freedom.

But that fragile peace was interrupted when, distantly to the north and west, they saw lantern lights burning, heard angry shouts.

"Shhh," Brian whispered. He grinned and set the point of his knife over Lamiya's heart. The rebel seemed almost buoyant, giddy. Kai could feel it from one-eared Olaf and Sophia as well: it was almost as if they were drunken with freedom.

The voices retreated to the west. The rebels whispered among themselves, then Tom Leary pointed east. "Look," he whispered. The eastern horizon blushed rose as the new sun prepared to greet the day. Brian sculled the boat into a sheltered little cove. "Aidan," he said. "You have first watch. Olaf, relieve him in three hours."

Brian covered himself with a blanket, curled up like a cat, and began snoring at once. Kai climbed over him to the back of the boat, carrying a water skin.

Lamiya's hands had been retied in front of her, and her face was unfettered; she had finally promised not to scream if they removed her gag. He thought that she looked tired and strained. At that moment, he would gladly have given his inheritance to comfort her, or free her from this nightmare.

"Here," he said, offering water. "You need this."

She caught the sides of the skin with her bound hands. "You are very friendly with them."

He shrugged. "Any animal caught in a trap will seek freedom."

She sipped again, as if just discovering the depth and intensity of her thirst. "We're going to die, aren't we?" Her tone was coldly matter-of-fact.

"No," Kai answered. *Don't lie to her, not now.* "Perhaps."

They sat together, sharing the quiet. "I'm cold," she said.

"It will be warmer soon."

"You could run. You could make it, Kai."

"I would never leave you alone."

She looked at him curiously, as if not entirely satisfied by his answer.

"Ali would be very displeased," he offered.

"Ah," she said. "Ali."

"Do you love my brother very much?"

Lamiya sighed. Then: "He is a good man. Our marriage unites two countries."

No answer at all, that. And yet in the pauses between her words, he sensed a meaning he dared not acknowledge. Both of them were weak, and tired. She was afraid, and in that mortal anguish would turn to whatever might comfort her. He was imagining things, that was all.

" 'It is low tide,' " he murmured, stirring his hand in the morning's cool water.

"Kai?"

He laughed. "Hafiz," he said.

"Ah." She closed her eyes with pleasure, lashes trembling against her cheek. "One of my favorite poets. Humor me."

Kai reflected for a moment, and then recited:

"Why all this talk of the beloved,
Music and dancing, and
Liquid ruby light we can lift in a cup?
Because it is low tide.
A very low tide in this age
And around most hearts."

Kai felt himself waver. Felt that he was speaking of things better left unsaid. Low tide, indeed. He could not help but continue:

"We are exquisite coral reefs,

Dying when exposed to strange
Elements.
Allah is the wine ocean we crave—we miss
Flowing in and out of our pores."

Kai paused, stopped. That was all he could say to her, even with the shelter of night. But to his surprise, she finished the poem, her voice a honeyed whisper.

"Find that flame, that existence
That wonderful man
Who can burn beneath the water.
No other kind of light
Will cook the food you need."

Kai could not breathe, could not speak. He had no label for the emotions he felt now. Could the slaves' mood be somehow, impossibly, infectious? He should have felt only horror and rage; his father was gravely wounded, perhaps dying! But somehow that fear was less than a sense of...freedom. Yes. There it was. Here, upon the river, he was just a man, without obligations, temporarily unable to control his fate and therefore not obliged to a responsibility for others.

He remembered Aidan's words, a dream that one day their children might play together. And his careless answer: *Freedom is a dream.* For Aidan? For himself?

Then what was this moment with Lamiya, so close to her that he could smell the salt of her skin mingling with soap and perfume. A chance for him to feel, even for a moment, that the two of them were together, separate from all obligations and controls, drifting in a tide of the heart.

Only in such a world could either of them possibly ignore the strictures that had guided them from birth.

Kai was suddenly, painfully, jarred by his own thoughts. What was he saying! His mind had strayed into a place of betrayal; of his brother, of his father's wishes, of Nandi's affections. And how presumptuous even to think that Lamiya could ever consider him as anything but a brother. He was deeply embarrassed, confused, prayed that she could not somehow read his heart. "Lamiya..." he finally said.

She was very close, both of them hidden in shadow. "Shhh."

He closed his eyes, vanquished by her single word.

Lamiya kissed him. It was not a sister's kiss.

Bharti Kirchner is the author of eight books—four novels and four cookbooks, and has been publishing since 1992. Her work has been translated into German, Dutch, Spanish, Marathi, Thai and other languages. Her novels include *Pastries: A Novel of Desserts and Discoveries, Darjeeling, Sharmila's Book,* and *Shiva Dancing* and cookbooks include *Indian Inspired* and *The Bold Vegetarian.* Bharti has written numerous articles and essays on food, travel, fitness, and lifestyle in magazines that include *Food & Wine, Eating Well, Vegetarian Times, The Writer, Writer's Digest, Fitness Plus,* and *Northwest Travel,* and book reviews for newspapers. Bharti has won two Seattle Arts Commission literature grants, and an Artist Trust GAP grant. She has been honored as a Living Pioneer Asian American Author.

Bharti read her story, *Food for the Goods,* at the 2009 Bedtime Stories event themed "In Your Dreams."

FOOD FOR THE GODS

Years ago, while dining out, I came across a dish on a restaurant menu called Kasha Varnishka, a mouthful of a name. My curiosity piqued, I decided to order it. A short time later, the waiter delivered a rustic brown pilaf-style dish. Made with a mysterious grain called kasha, it was mixed with caramelized onions, peas and, surprisingly, small pasta. The grain seemed light, almost ethereal to my palate at first, then gained a heavier, substantial quality and, finally, imparted a hint of bitterness.

A winner of a dish, I concluded. But what was it?

That evening, I went home full and satisfied, but my mind buzzed with questions. Where did the dish originate? Why wasn't kasha widely known as a grain? How could I learn to prepare it at home?

These were pre-Internet days, so I couldn't just Google kasha and instantly know all there was to know about it. I went to the library and combed the stacks. My research revealed that grain-like kasha was actually the seed of the buckwheat plant, not a grass like rice or wheat. That made it even more appealing and exotic to me. Nor only did kasha contain more protein than most grains, but also it had a richer profile in iron and potassium. To someone like me, born and raised on rice, wheat, and barley, the buckwheat groat presented itself as an exciting new grain-substitute.

As a cook, I find grains exciting. Historically, they've been known as the building blocks of civilizations. Rice has been revered as a staple in Asia for millennia, wheat has long nourished European nations, and quinoa is said to have been responsible for the rise of the Incas.

Another intriguing aspect of the dish was the presence of varnishka, or bow-tie pasta, a fresh concept in cooking. Combine a protein-rich seed with a high carb ingredient and render it even more nourishing. Who thought of it?

More trips to the library. Soon I learned that the dish had originated in the kitchens of Eastern Europe and was well loved in that part of the world.

Eager to find out more, I asked around. None of my friends had ever cooked with whole buckwheat kernels. A few had used buckwheat flour to make pancakes or enjoyed it in the form of soba noodles in Japanese restaurants, but that was about all.

Soon my dreams were filled with vignettes about kasha. It haunted me at dinner and every time I walked the aisles of the grocery store. I wanted to meet with a cook from Eastern Europe, who'd actually made the dish, but knew of no one with that background.

Then it occurred to me: in the apartment building where I lived, we had a superintendent who was Czech. It'd be simple enough to ask her, but therein lay a problem. Mrs. Vesely had a surly disposition. She routinely ignored her tenants' pleas for repair work—a stuck window, a burned oven light, or creaky bathroom door. The faucet in my kitchen had been leaking for a week and had worn me down with its dripping sounds, not to mention the guilt I'd been feeling for wasting precious water. But she'd done nothing to fix it. I'd asked her three times and finally had stopped, frustrated by my inability to have a pleasant conversation with her.

But, once again, my curiosity got the best of me and so, one evening, I finally mustered up my courage and knocked on her door. I trembled inwardly as I waited.

No answer. I was about to turn away when the door swung open. Before me stood a tall stocky woman, with fierce eyes, whose tight curls seemed to burst out in all directions. She looked like someone who had been disturbed in the middle of a deep sleep and was irritated beyond belief. Yet, she couldn't have been sleeping. A warm fragrance radiated from her kitchen. Her apron was splattered with dark brownish spots. It was obvious that she'd been cooking. That seemed like a good sign to me.

"What do you want now?" Mrs. Vesely snapped.

I forced a smile and humbly enquired about kasha.

She gave me an intense look of disbelief. "Kasha?" she replied in a reverential tone. "You're asking about kasha?"

"Yes, yes."

Her face relaxed, her eyes glowed, and she blew a kiss in the air. "It's a food fit for the gods."

Thus encouraged, I pressed on. "Please tell me more. I'd like to make a dish gods like to eat."

"Long story," she said.

Standing there spellbound, I listened. Back home, it turned out, not only did she regularly prepare kasha varnishka, but also tossed handfuls of kasha in soups, stews, or whatever happened to be simmering on the stove. Her son, Milan, had the ruddiest cheeks in town and her daughter, Sabine, could jump higher than any girl her age. Alas, the children were grown and had left home. Now that she lived alone here in the U.S., there was no need to stock the pantry shelf with boxes of buckwheat groats, the original high-energy staple, the food gods were believed to consume, the food that nourished both body and soul of mere mortals. She hadn't prepared kasha in years.

No wonder, I thought, she never smiled.

"You're the first person ever to mention it," she mused wistfully. "No one I know eats kasha. Our cooking is unknown here."

"I'm going to change that."

"But you're Indian. Why would you cook something so foreign?"

"I like to try new things in the kitchen."

I could have told her more. That food can transcend borders. That cooks speak a universal language. That you make friends at the dinner table, not enemies. That variety is the essence of life.

"So, you think you can cook kasha varnishka?" she asked.

"Why don't you just wait and see?"

She fixed me with a skeptical stare, then proceeded to give me basic instructions for preparing the dish.

She'd indeed thrown a challenge at me.

The next day after work I stopped at the corner supermarket, bought a box of Wolf's buckwheat groats and a few other items, and hurried home. After tossing my suit jacket onto a chair in the living room, I went straight to the kitchen. I was still wearing my favorite rose-pink silk blouse. The notion of taking time to change out of my corporate uniform or don an apron never occurred to me. I was too busy thinking about how to get the dish right.

As I began sautéing a generous amount of onion in a skillet, a savory aroma perfumed the air. Heady with anticipation, I then added the main ingredient, brownish buckwheat kernels coated with a beaten egg. Next, I added boiling water. I watched as the kernels puffed up and released a nutty fragrance. On another burner, in a kettle of bubbling water, I boiled bowtie-shaped varnishka. Soon they popped up to the surface, glistening like miniature ivory carvings. Once the varnishka softened, I drained and tossed them with the kasha pilaf, arranged it all in a platter, and garnished the result with parsley. Then I looked down at my blouse.

Oh, no. It was spotted with blemishes caused by the sputtering of hot oil.

Finally, I took a taste of the finished dish. Soft textured, nutty flavored, and bursting with goodness, it was so splendid, so warming to my belly, so satisfying to my palate that I forgot all about the demise of my blouse. I pegged it as a dish for company, one that could be served as the main attraction. Or it could be a side show to be paired with either meat or meatless entrées.

But I wasn't done quite yet. I packed a generous portion in a Tupperware for my landlady and buzzed her doorbell.

The same gruff babushka swung the door open, but before she could bark out her usual question, I thrust the container into her hand.

"I made some kasha for you, if you'd care to try."

She sniffed, looked up, mumbled something joyously in Czech, and invited me in. Then, after an initial taste, she blew a kiss in my direction.

"Oh, my, this is just like back home," she murmured, dreamy-eyed.

A long conversation ensued. We discussed recipes, family, festivities, and whether the small or medium kasha was superior for cooking purposes. We were like old friends, disagreeing at first about the size of the kernels, then both voting for the medium size. She even confided that her last name, Vesely, meant "cheerful," which I'd have thought a contradiction even a week ago, but not any more.

The very next day a plumber showed up to fix the leaky faucet in my kitchen. And, from then on, my "cheerful" landlady spoke to me kindly, as though I was someone with whom she shared a common bond. My friends appreciated the hearty dish as well, a fancy noodle casserole as one of them called it. No, it was much more than that, insisted another.

Despite these splendid results, it pained me that my pink blouse was ruined forever. No dry cleaner in the city could remove the oil stains from its delicate silk threads. After a time I accepted the fact that the garment was beyond saving. It hung in the back of my closet, still exquisite-looking, a memento of the joy of experimenting in the kitchen. It reminded me of the magic of listening, of making friends across cultures.

If kasha hasn't built a civilization yet, it has at least won me a neighbor's goodwill. It has broken down a barrier and replaced it with a solid connection. For that I'll forever remain grateful to it.

Photo Copyright © James Alred.

A poet, novelist, short story writer, and essayist, Jana Harris's award-winning books include *Manhattan as a Second Language and Other Poems* (Harper & Row) and *Oh How Can I Keep On Singing?: Voices of Pioneer Women* (Ontario Press, Princeton), both Pulitzer Prize nominees. *Oh How Can I Keep On Singing?* was a Washington State Governor's Writers Award winner, a PEN West Center Award finalist, and has been adapted for educational television. Harris is founder and editor of Switched-on Gutenberg, one of the first online poetry journals and teaches poetry and creative writing online at the University of Washington and at thewritersworkshop.net. She lives in the foothills of the Cascades where she and her husband raise horses. A memoir, *Horses Never Lie*, is forthcoming.

The story "Stone Lambs" was written while researching a play about the life of immigration activist Grace Abbott. Jana read *Stone Lambs* at the 2007 Bedtime Stories event themed "Night Light."

STONE LAMBS

Franklin "Lucky" Tubbs Recalls July, 1887

We climbed out of the ship's darkness. My hand a small pink seashell in her much larger hand. With her other arm Mother cradled the sleeping baby in the space between her neck and shoulder. He was the size and softness of a loaf of bread.

Suddenly everyone started shouting and the rancid fat smell of the hold disappeared. One of my sisters lifted me up to see a tall lady the color of the sun rising out of the harbor. I would have been frightened if my mother hadn't been so happy. She adjusted her black scarf, checked its hard knot under her chin. The harbor lady wore a strange head scarf of many spikes. The triangle of Mother's scarf had only three, none as sharp as the harbor lady's. Mother pointed: See her torch. A statue of a schoolteacher? one of the girls asked. Another said: Maybe in America, this is the Virgin Mary. Everyone was yelling the one English word we all knew, *America*. The sea filled with diamonds; my eyes felt weak. It had been so hot below that I had cried all night. Men had smoked their pipes, which made my tears sting.

The crowd pushed toward the bow. I was just a tiny tot unused to walking very far, so I grabbed the hem of Mother's black coat next to a clot of coins she'd sewn inside it. Don't let go or I'll lose you forever, she said.

A tugboat met our steamer and an immigration inspector came aboard to see if any of us were diseased. We walked single file past him. Our baby cried and soon began to wail. The immigration officer had the meaty face of boiled brisket; I felt so hungry. He stared at Mother, then at the baby. The man seemed not to notice me, a good boy too young to speak, but old enough to know better than to bleat at the top of his lungs. With a string of consonants, the officer waved us along. We stood in another line for so long that I began to think Mother looked like the colossal lady.

All seven hundred of us aboard were taken by flat-bottomed barge to a pier where a mountain of luggage loomed at a frightful angle. Finally one of the girls found our trunk, which we stood beside, until a bald customs agent approached. He unbuckled each leather strap, tossed our belongings with a stick, closed the lid, and struck the top with a white chalk line.

Next we were herded into open wagons and taken with our trunk to the Immigrant Depot. Larger than a steamship out of water, the stone fort had circular walls and massive beams. Inside, we again stood in line. Raising my arms, I begged Mother or one of the girls to pick me up. The baby continued to cry. What had happened to my father? I've no memory of him, just a vague image of a man in a hat.

We were prodded into an endless narrow hall, walls as high as the icebergs our ship had sailed past. Slowly we approached a tall cadaverous inspector whose blue uniform smelled like wet sheepskin. He said something we couldn't understand, then motioned Mother and the girls to pass. Pulling me aside, he studied my red swollen eyes. A clerk with a huge head and short arms held me while another clerk in a white coat pulled at my eyelids again and again with a silver button hook. In between times he consulted a manual. "Paving stone appearance," he wrote. "Evidence of granulation." He cleared his throat: "Sandy Blight." Later this was translated for us. He waved me along.

Mother waited for our paperwork to be stamped *Admitted*. Instead, an inspector grabbed her arm, pushing us into a shorter line that led to a room where people lay on their coats on the stone floor.

Why could we not continue out the iron gate into the city streets like everyone else? Mother did not understand. She had train tickets for Chicago. I had seen her show them to the women aboard ship. The baby wailed. My sisters stared at their hard black shoes. The cadaverous man stamped our paperwork *Detained*.

Finally after the sun had set in the small windows way up near the roofline, a translator, Mr. Becker, was located. Fine-boned as a child with limp colorless hair, he would not stop staring at me. He stood between a doctor and a customs officer as he told Mother that I would have to be sent to a hospital until my eyes healed. It might take months. Otherwise, the immigration doctor said, that it was likely my eyes wouldn't ever heal, that I would go blind, and spread Trachoma to every American.

"Trachoma?" Mother's brow creased.

Mr. Becker continued as if she hadn't spoken: I could not be admitted to the United States, he told her.

The United States? We had boarded a ship for America. Worse, my mother had no money for a hospital. She had our train tickets.

Did we have landing money? A sponsor? Could a relative be located? There was a lot of head shaking.

It seemed that, because of my eyes, I would be *excluded*, sent back on the steamer's return trip. The law said that the shipping company would have to pay. I was barely three, too young to go alone, so Mother would have to accompany me and pay a fare. Now both she and the baby cried. My sisters started to cry. They rubbed their noses on the pointed ties of their scarves, which wilted. While all this was going on, Mr. Becker continued to stare at me, his small pig eyes rooting holes in my chest.

In the end, Mother, the baby, and the girls were admitted. I was detained in the immigrant hospital. Mr. Becker helped Mother sell the railroad tickets to pay for a month of cure. Even though the brick hospital felt stark, I was given a blanket and my own bed; the first time I'd ever slept alone, which frightened me. I cried all the time. My eyes became more inflamed. Every morning a nurse rubbed my inner lids with bluestone, a stick of powdery copper which burned worse than a cinder and turned my eyes from red to crimson.

Each time Mother visited, the smudges beneath her eyes looked darker. I was in an upstairs ward with other detained children. A girl who'd had measles onboard our ship now had developed Bright's Disease; a boy who'd tripped on deck and hurt his leg, the wound turning septic. The nurses were bent, grandmotherly women. The doctor, a corpulent man with a belly larger than St. Nick's, was not at all jolly, his face so red it verged on purple. The girl with the diseased kidneys caught scarlet fever and our ward was quarantined from the other children who suffered a variety of complaints: favus, ringworm, brain dropsy.

When, after a month, my eyes showed no improvement and Mother had no more money to pay for my cure, the doctor raised his hand to mark my paperwork *Deported*. Mother cried bitterly. My sisters remained outside in the street caring for the baby. Mr. Becker, who always seemed to be lurking nearby, said he had a solution. He knew of a charitable family who would take me in—part of an auxiliary to the Immigrant Benevolent Society.

Mother asked if she had heard him correctly. I hadn't seen the ivory buttons of her smile since we arrived here. The agreement was that Mr. Becker would send for Mother when I was cured, but until then, the sheltering family was not to be disturbed.

* * *

That's how I came to live with Mr. and Mrs. Tubbs in the brownstone on Joraleman Street. Their house—almost as big as the hospital—had a copper elm in front, a gardener's cottage in back, and a mews in the alley. Inside, every window was covered with white veils. My room upstairs overflowed with toys and looked as if I had always lived there. I had a rocking pony with a real horse's mane and tail; a cannon that shot real balls; lead soldiers I thought were customs agents painted blue and gray. The most magnificent thing was a portrait of me inside a heavy gold frame that hung on the wall.

At home I'd amused myself in the cellar with potato sacks, thumped the squashes kept in bins. I missed the dark smell of fresh earth. Except for the hospital, I'd never been in a building with a second story, let alone been asked to sleep in a room by myself.

They called me Frankie. Helga, the maid, called me Lucky, so did the neighbor ladies who visited Mrs. Tubbs. I liked Helga, she had a face as flat as a cookie and hair like whipped egg whites. Verity, Mrs. Tubbs, looked like a doll with hair as fine as corn silk. She was taking the rest cure and stayed in bed. When Poppa first brought me to her room, she sat up amid her satin sheets with an excited expression. "Oh, there you are," she said in a breathy voice. "I've been waiting for you for the longest time."

Poppa, a jovial man with a huge red mustache, managed a crutch and cane manufacturing company owned by his father-in-law, Colonel Franklin, who'd suffered a stroke of paralysis. When Poppa went to work, he wore a tall black hat and carried a shiny black stick.

The affliction in my eyes vanished. I was allowed out of my room, dressed in short pants and a plaited blouse trimmed with a leather belt. Meanwhile, I'd begun to talk and to learn English. I waited for Mother, eager to show her how well I could ask to be picked up. No longer would I have to raise my arms. Every time Helga answered the door, I stood ready with my lead soldiers in my pockets. I'd grown to like playing with them and didn't want to leave them behind.

I was allowed in Verity's room but a few times a week. My visits over-excited her, Helga said. I warmed to Verity; she let me watch her while she crocheted doilies. Hundreds of them littered the house. They reminded me of snowflakes and I found them strangely comforting. Sometimes I snuck into her room and we played with her porcelain miniatures which she kept in a glass case. "I have the entire Spanish Habsburg Court," she told me, "including Prince Balthazar."

Daily I would watch for my chance to get in to see her and play with the Prince and his regents. All these years later, I'll never forget how she cocked her little sparrow face and said, "You know, you do look just like him." She was my only playmate. I watched as men with black bags came and went from her room mumbling to Helga.

Once while Poppa was smoking a cigar with his feet propped up on a carpeted stool, I asked him about my mother. "She's upstairs," he told me, blowing a gray cloud that floated to the ceiling in the shape of a question mark. "The doctor prescribed something to help her rest."

Not Verity, I told him, *my mother.* When would she come for me as Mr. Becker had told her to?

Poppa's square body jerked upright. His face grew pink, his cheeks ballooned. "Your mother's upstairs," he said sternly. "Never mention your life before you entered this house. Verity's delicate. Don't you dare hurt her." With his arm like a yard stick, he swung at me, his fingernails catching me across the nose.

I fell to the floor, terrified. I began to wail. Helga ran in and picked me up, pressing my face into the stiff white apron that covered her black dress.

"I cannot abide an ungrateful child," Poppa told her.

I didn't want to harm the doll-like lady in bed upstairs, so was afraid to ask when my mother would come, afraid to say much of anything after that.

Poppa had a library in his smoking room, and I began to teach myself to read, but with much difficulty, so mostly I looked at atlases trying to find Chicago. I would often try to sneak into Verity's room with one and ask her about the place names. "Oh, what fun," she said. "Let me show you where Prince Balthazar lived." Even her smile smelled like lilacs. I ached to remember my life before coming to the house on Joraleman, but slowly, as I learned to speak English, it faded from memory.

One day when I was just grammar school age, I stopped at the window, contemplating the curtain panels, each a sheer piece of lace like the wedding train that hung in Verity's closet—if I was good, she would let me stroke it. Then I noticed a woman lingering in front of our brownstone. My eyes flew to the scarf on her head, the knot under her chin. That tilt of the triangle that covered her hair, how it angled away from her forehead instead of sheltering her. It was as if her face were a lantern into a day I had not realized had been dark. For some reason I recalled the morning I had emerged from the ship's hold to see the colossal copper lady holding a book and a torch.

The woman on the street—sturdy as an elm and tall as a man— walked up our sandstone steps. I held my breath as I heard the clap of the brass door knocker. Helga answered. I crouched in a recess off the entryway where coats were hung out of sight. What voice told me to lie low, I knew not.

She spoke to Helga in broken English. After a garbled "hello," I couldn't make out the rest of her sentence, but I think it was a question. Helga spoke sharply: *scat*, she said as she would to one of the hungry cats that begged kitchen scraps. "Valdyslaw," screamed the woman. The door banged shut in her face. When Helga spun around and saw me standing there she burst into tears, scooped me into her arms, and ran up the stairs, locking me in my room.

That voice, I knew it. *Valdyslaw*, rang in my ears.

I banged on my bedroom door and when that didn't work, I kicked it and pounded the parquet floor tiles. Pulling the sheets off my bed, I tore them with my teeth. Valdyslaw had been my name.

Poppa was sent for. When he arrived, he told me, "Frankie, you'll damage your mother's health if you carry on any longer." But that had been my mother at the door, the woman Helga had chased away like a stray.

After that, on my way to school—always accompanied by Helga— we walked a different route each day through the park. Black swans patrolled the pond where I sailed the boat I'd been given for my birthday. Whenever I saw a woman sitting on a park bench wearing a triangle scarf tied with a strong well-proportioned knot under her chin and a certain look in her feathery hazel eyes, I was filled with longing.

That was also when I began to recall shadows of my past. Poppa called them nightmares. "If you don't stop screaming in the wee hours, you'll kill your mother," he roared.

I could not. My name wasn't Frankie or Frank or even Franklin. The dreams had begun when I'd heard my mother's voice calling my name, too big a mouthful for a tot to say or even remember. In my sleep I saw bending wheat grass, a village, the thatched roof of our tiny house sitting low to a street rutted with mud and clogged with carts. We must have lived in a cellar, because I recall the smell of damp clay and a bin of hard squash, sacks of potatoes, and spiders that wove endless beautiful white webs.

In another dream, I was sitting with Mother on the porch in sunlight as she tied white threads, knotting them into a strange geometry of flowers and birds. There wasn't room for me in Mother's lap; under her apron was a squash, or something like it. When I thumped her lap it made the same thudding noise as when I knocked on a squash. Soon a lump of dough appeared in our bed. Mostly it slept, but often it wailed.

I remembered rain, the street ruts deepening, droplets making rings in vast puddles. The mud turned absolutely black. Across the street, the porch roofs sagged. There was a house of wooden panels trussed with crossrails, like x's, and a crossbuck door. I recalled so clearly those wooden x's. A man stood in front of the door across the muddy street where I was told never to wander. The man had a beard and wore a hat. Soldiers came riding down the street on black horses, their legs as thin as my mother's arm, their knees raised high, manes and tails blowing like flags. I had never seen anything so god-like as those horses.

A cavalry officer stopped in front of the door where the man lingered. The officer patted his horse's neck with one gloved hand, then drew a long knife from the side of his belt and slashed an x across the neck of the man who stood motionless. The soldier spurred his horse and trotted away. Slowly the man fell to his knees. Red gushed out of his throat and down the front of his collarless shirt.

I don't remember anything else, other than being on the boat, tiers of berths with many people on each mattress, a dark hold more crowded than our cellar had ever been. Waves as tall as houses rocked us. My stomach rose into the back of my mouth. Vomit was everywhere, everyone's mixing together. All I wanted was a drink of water.

* * *

Every time I dreamed of the man with a red x slashed into his throat, I woke up in a screaming sweat. Helga rushed into my room to quiet me so that Verity wouldn't hear.

About six months after my mother had appeared at the door, things started going wrong at the crutch and cane factory. Poppa had to discharge workers. The word "bankruptcy" rattled the downstairs windows. Men with hair that looked chewed by dogs knocked at our door. A week later when old Colonel Franklin died, Poppa stared at me as if I'd taken a kitchen knife and drawn an x across his father-in-law's throat.

I kept hearing Mr. and Mrs. Tubbs arguing behind her bedroom door. "I don't want you to go to the cemetery," Poppa told his wife. "You know how upset you got the last time." Doctors came and went, delivering prescriptions for Verity. Whenever I snuck in to see her, the doll-lady was so fast asleep that I could not wake her.

"The poor grieving woman," Helga said. She didn't think that I should go to Colonel Franklin's funeral either, but Poppa insisted: I was a big boy; besides, I had been named for the old man. I wanted to be big, but knew better than to remind him that I already had a name. We sat in a black carriage as shiny as a rooster's tail, lanterns lit though it was a sunny morning in August. No one spoke. Helga held my hand, my fist balled like a rock. The coachman rode up top as the hearse horse clomped. I wondered if Prince Balthazar had ever ridden in such finery.

As grownups gathered around Colonel Franklin's open grave, I sat down next to a stone lamb and caressed its soothing marble back, its little cloven hooves, the stub of its tail. I kissed its bald eyes, my fingers tracing the swirls of a stone ruff around its neck. In the sun, its body felt surprisingly warm. At any moment the lamb might nibble my hand.

Then I noticed writing below the lamb's chest. Chiseled into the white marble was my American name. Franklin Tubbs: Born on my birthday party day. Died 1887. My breath stopped. My eyes refused to unfasten themselves from the headstone. Suddenly I felt the cold waters of the Atlantic pour over my head.

The mourners threw handfuls of dirt into the grave. No one saw me slip away. I ran as long as I could and finally reached the pilings of the Brooklyn docks. The granite towers and looping cables of the celebrated bridge looked like a perilous contrivance. With all the power within me I willed myself to cross, then walked for endless blocks in her direction.

I had not seen the colossal copper lady since that day on the steamer. If I was going to find my mother, I had to know what she looked like: The heavy brow, the straight flat nose, the well-muscled arms. The statue was still the color of the sun, but green tears now ran down her cheeks. I sat at the water's edge and stared into the harbor at her torch, her book, the spikes of her head scarf.

What did I know about myself? First name: Valdyslaw. Surname: Known but to God. Country of origin: Where the black earth of the steppe was patched with strips of wheat, square thatched dwellings, and hardly a tree. Father: dead. Mother: lacemaker. Arrived in the United States: 1887 aboard the *S.S. Unremembered.*

Then I began to wonder: What had happened to the rest of them, the other infirm, detained, and excluded children? There must have been an army of us. Lambs without language or history or name; our pockets empty, except for one single word of English—that gold coin, that light unto our path, *America.*

This story is dedicated to Judith Johnson and to Harry Smith.

Photo Copyright © Mary Randlett.

Charles Johnson is a former trustee of Humanities Washington, a 1998 MacArthur Fellow and a Professor (Emeritus) of English at the University of Washington. He is the author of several books, including *Faith and the Good Thing*, and winner of the 1990 National Book Award for *Middle Passage*. He has read at every Bedtime Stories event and had a collection of his works composed for the event entitled *Dr. King's Refrigerator*.

As the founding father of Humanities Washington's Bedtime Stories event, Charles has created and read an original story each year since the event began in 1999. He read his story, *Dr. King's Refrigerator*, at the 2002 event themed "Midnight Snack."

DR. KING'S REFRIGERATOR

अन्नद् भवन्ति भुतानि

"Beings exist from food."
Bhagavad-Gita, Book 3, Chapter 14

In September, the year of Our Lord 1954, a gifted, young minister from Atlanta named Martin Luther King Jr., accepted his first pastorate at the Dexter Avenue Baptist Church in Montgomery, Alabama. He was twenty-five-years old, and in the language of the Academy he took his first job when he was ABD at Boston University's School of Theology—*All But Dissertation*—which is a common and necessary practice for scholars who have completed their coursework and have families to feed. If you are offered a job when still in graduate school, you snatch it and, if all goes well, you finish the thesis that first year of your employment when you are in the thick of things, trying mightily to prove—in Martin's case— to the staid, high-toned laity at Dexter that you really are worth the $4,800 salary they were paying you. He had, by the way, the highest-paying job of any minister in the city of Montgomery, and the expectations for his daily performance—as a pastor, husband, community leader, and the son of Daddy King—were equally high.

But what few people tell the eager ABD is how completing the doctorate from a distance means wall-to-wall work. There were always meetings with the local NAACP, ministers' organizations, and church committees; or, failing that, the budget and treasury to balance; or, failing that, the sick to visit in their homes, the ordination of deacons to preside over, and a new sermon to write *every* week. During that first year away from Boston, he delivered forty-six sermons to his congregation, and twenty sermons and lectures at other colleges and churches in the South. And, dutifully, he got up every morning at 5:30 to spend three hours composing the thesis in his parsonage, a white frame house with a railed-in front porch and two oak trees in the yard, after which he devoted another three hours to it late at night, in addition to spending sixteen hours each week on his Sunday sermons.

On the Wednesday night of December first, exactly one year before Rosa Parks refused to give up her bus seat, and after a long day of meetings, writing memos and letters, he sat entrenched behind a roll-top desk in his cluttered den at five minutes past midnight, smoking cigarettes and drinking black coffee, wearing an old fisherman's knit sweater, his desk barricaded in by books and piles of paperwork. Naturally, his in-progress dissertation, "A Comparison of the Conceptions of God in the Thinking of Paul Tillich and Henry Nelson Wieman," was itching at the edge of his mind, but what he really needed this night was a theme for his sermon on Sunday. Usually, by Tuesday Martin at least had a sketch, by Wednesday he had his research and citations—which ranged freely over five thousand years of Eastern and Western philosophy—compiled on note cards, and by Friday he was writing his text on a pad of lined, yellow paper. Put bluntly, he was two days behind schedule.

A few rooms away, his wife was sleeping under a blue corduroy bedspread. For an instant he thought of giving up work for the night and climbing into sheets warmed by her body, curling up beside this heartbreakingly beautiful and very understanding woman, a graduate of the New England Conservatory of Music, who had sacrificed her career back east in order to follow him into the Deep South. He remembered their wedding night on June 18th a year ago in Perry County, Alabama, and how the insanity of segregation meant he and his new bride could not stay in a hotel operated by whites. Instead, they spent their wedding night at a black funeral home and had no honeymoon at all. Yes, he probably *should* join her in their bedroom. He wondered if she resented how his academic and theological duties took him away from her and their home (Many an ABD's marriage ended before the dissertation was done)—work like that infernal, unwritten sermon, which hung over his head like the sword of Damocles.

Weary, feeling guilty, he pushed back from his desk, stretched out his stiff spine, and decided to get a midnight snack.

Now, he *knew* he shouldn't do that, of course. He often told friends that food was his greatest weakness. His ideal weight in college was 150 pounds, and he was aware that, at 5 feet, 7 inches tall, he should not eat between meals. His bantam weight ballooned easily. Moreover, he'd read somewhere that the average American will in his (or her) lifetime eat 60,000 pounds of food. To Martin's ethical way of thinking, consuming that much tonnage was downright obscene, given the fact that there was so much famine and poverty throughout the rest of the world. He made himself a promise—a small prayer—to eat just a little, only enough tonight to replenish his tissues.

He made his way cautiously through the dark, seven-room house, his footsteps echoing on the hardwood floors like he was in a swimming pool, scuffing from the smoke-filled den to the living room, where he circled round the baby grand piano his wife practiced on for church recitals, then past her choices in decorations—two African masks on one wall and West Indian gourds on the mantle above the fireplace—to the kitchen. There, he clicked on the overhead light, and drew open the door to their refrigerator.

Scratching his stomach, he gazed—and gazed—at four, well-stocked shelves of food. He saw a Florida grapefruit and a California orange. On one of the middle shelves he saw corn and squash, both native to North America, and introduced by Indians to Europe in the fifteenth century through Columbus. To the right of that, his eyes tracked bright yellow slices of pineapple from Hawaii, truffles from England and a half-eaten Mexican *tortilla*. Martin took a step back, cocking his head to one side, less hungry now than curious about what his wife had found at public market, and stacked inside their refrigerator without telling him.

He began to empty the refrigerator and heavily-packed food cabinets, placing everything on the table and kitchen counter and, when those were filled, on the flower-printed linoleum floor, taking things out slowly at first, his eyes squinted, scrutinizing each item like an old woman on a fixed budget at the bargain table in a grocery store. Then he worked quickly, bewitched, chuckling to himself as he tore apart his wife's tidy, well-scrubbed, Christian kitchen. He removed all the beryline olives from a thick, glass jar and held each one up to the light, as if perhaps he'd never really *seen* an olive before, or seen one so clearly. Of one thing he was sure: no two olives were the same. Within fifteen minutes, Martin stood surrounded by a galaxy of food.

From one corner of the kitchen floor to the other, there were popular American items such as pumpkin pie and hotdogs, but also heavy, sour-sweet dishes like German sauerkraut and *schnitzel* right beside Tibetan rice, one of the staples of the Far East, all sorts of spices, and the macaroni, spaghetti, and ravioli favored by Italians. There were bricks of cheese and wine from French vineyards, coffee from Brazil, and from China and India black and green teas that probably had been carried from fields to far away markets on the heads of women, or the backs of donkeys, horses and mules. All of human culture, history and civilization lie unscrolled at his feet, and he had only to step into his kitchen to discover it. No one people or tribe, living in one place on this planet, could produce the endless riches for the palate that he'd just pulled from his refrigerator. He looked around the disheveled room, and he saw in each succulent fruit, each slice of bread, and each grain of rice a fragile, inescapable network of mutuality in which all earthly creatures were co-dependent, integrated, and tied in a single garment of destiny. He recalled Exodus 25:30, and realized all this before him was showbread. From the floor Martin picked up a Golden Delicious apple, took a bite from it, and instantly he prehended the haze of heat from summers past, the roots of the tree from which the fruit was taken, the cycles of sun and rain and seasons, the earth and even those who tended the orchard. Then he slowly put the apple down, feeling not so much hunger now as a profound indebtedness and thanksgiving—— to everyone and everything in Creation. For was not *he*, too, the product of infinite causes and the full, miraculous orchestration of Being stretching back to the beginning of time?

At that moment his wife came into the disaster area that was their kitchen, half-asleep, wearing blue slippers and an old housecoat over her nightgown. When she saw what her philosopher husband had done, she said, *Oh!* And promptly disappeared from the room. A moment later, she was back, having composed herself and put her glasses on, but her voice was barely above a whisper:

"Are you all right?"

"Of course, I am! I've *never* felt better!" he said. "The whole universe is inside our refrigerator!"

She blinked.

"Really? You don't mean that, do you? Honey, have you been drinking? I've told you time and again that orange juice and vodka you like so much isn't good for you, and if anyone at church smells it on your breath..."

"If you *must* know, I was hard at work on my thesis an hour ago. I didn't drink a drop of *anything*—except coffee."

"Well, that explains," she said.

"No, you don't understand! I was trying to write my speech for Sunday, but—but—I couldn't think of anything, and I got hungry..."

She stared at food heaped on the floor. "*This* hungry?"

"Well, *no.*" His mouth wobbled, and now he was no longer thinking about the metaphysics of food but instead how the mess he'd made must look through her eyes. And, more importantly, how *he* must look through her eyes. "I think I've got my sermon, or at least something I might use later. It's so obvious to me now!" He could tell by the tilt of her head and twitching of her nose that she didn't think any of this was obvious at all. "When we get up in the morning, we go into the bathroom where we reach for a sponge provided for us by a Pacific Islander. We reach for soap created by a Frenchman. The towel is provided by a Turk. Before we leave for our jobs, we are beholden to more than half the world."

"Yes, dear." She sighed. "I can *see* that, but what about my kitchen? You *know* I'm hosting the Ladies Prayer Circle today at eight o'clock. That's seven hours from now. Please tell me you're going to clean up everything before you go to bed."

"But I have a sermon to write! What I'm saying—*trying* to say—is that whatever affects *one* directly, affects *all* indirectly!"

"Oh, yes, I'm sure all this is going to have a remarkable affect on the Ladies Prayer Circle..."

"Sweetheart..." he held up a grapefruit and a head of lettuce, "I had a *revelation* tonight. Do you know how rare that is? Those things don't come easy. Just ask Meister Eckhart or Martin Luther—you know Luther experienced enlightenment on the toilet, don't you? Ministers only get maybe one or two revelations in a lifetime. But *you* made it possible for me to have a vision when I opened the refrigerator." All at once, he had a discomforting thought. "How much *did* you spend for groceries last week?"

"I bought extra things for the Ladies Prayer Circle," she said. "Don't ask how much and I won't ask why you've turned the kitchen inside-out." Gracefully, like an angel, or the perfect wife in the Book of Proverbs, she stepped toward him over cans and containers, plates of leftovers and bowls of chili. She placed her hand on his cheek, like a mother might do with her gifted and exasperating child, a prodigy who had just torched his bedroom in a scientific experiment. Then she wrapped her arms around him, slipped her hands under his sweater, and gave him a good, long kiss—by the time they were finished her glasses were fogged. Stepping back, she touched the tip of his nose with her finger, and turned to leave. "Don't stay up too late," she said. "Put everything back before it spoils. And come to bed—I'll be waiting."

Martin watched her leave and said, "Yes, dear," still holding a very spiritually understood grapefruit in one hand and an ontologically clarified head of lettuce in the other. He started putting back everything on the shelves, deciding as he did so that while his sermon could wait until morning, his new wife definitely should not.

Photo courtesy of Krysta Ficca.

Daniel Orozco's work has appeared in *Best American Essays, Best American Short Stories, Best American Mystery Stories* and *Pushcart Prize* anthologies, and in *Harper's Magazine, McSweeney's, Zoetrope,* and others. He is the recipient of a National Endowment for the Arts fellowship. He teaches in the Creative Writing Program at the University of Idaho.

Dan read his story, *Cuore Inverno,* at the 2008 event themed "Night Hawk."

CUORE INVERNO

They were on a blind date, arranged by a friend she worked with whose husband knew him. They had been chatting in the wine bar, waiting for a table at a popular Italian café that did not take reservations. They had been waiting over an hour, but neither of them seemed to mind, and their patience was rewarded with an intimate table, tucked into an alcove whose windows looked out on a tiny lantern-lit garden. There were long waits between menus and ordering, between salads and entrees, but they both seemed to relish the leisurely pace, which allowed the conversation to carom pleasantly from subject to subject. This was her favorite part of a date—its first few hours, when the pretense of best behavior held sway and the blemishes of individual personality had yet to appear. So things were going well. But, after they ordered dessert, the subject of movies came up.

She told him about an old western she had just seen. The previous week she had been laid up with a stomach flu, unable to move or eat for days, and she watched TV the whole time. The hero was a cavalry officer and throughout the movie he had been shooting Indians out of their saddles without batting an eye. But when he had to kill his lame horse, the hero—one of those archetypal western stoics—became hesitant and dewy-eyed.

"His name was Ol' Blue," she said. "Or Ol' Buck. The horse, I mean. And damn if I didn't start crying. It's nothing to watch people die, but when the horse gets it, I'm all weepy. Isn't that awful?"

"Not so awful," her date said. "The Indians were the bad guys. You were supposed to not care. That's how they made movies back then."

She nodded. "It still bothers me, though. People can die by the dozen, but it only gets to me when a horse or a dog is caught in the crossfire. You know what I mean?"

"I do." He leaned toward her. "I *do* know what you mean. But you see, dogs are innocent. People deserve to get it. The bad ones, anyway."

"I know," she said. The flame of a candle flickered between them. She watched the light play on his face. "Sometimes I worry that I'm hardened to it. Watching human beings die while munching on popcorn."

"I don't think that would be possible with you," he said. "To be hardened, I mean."

She twirled her wine glass, looked into it and smiled. A comfy silence arose. Dinnerware clattered quietly around them. A siren in the distance rose and fell, rose and fell.

"But then," he said, "that would depend on the human being, wouldn't it?"

She asked him what he meant. Before answering, he reached for the wine bottle, topped off her glass, and refilled his own. He leaned back in his chair.

"Let's say you're in a room," he said. "In one corner, there's a dog, and in the other corner, a man. A man who has killed without remorse." He sipped from his glass. She waited, her mouth slightly open.

"You have a gun," he said. "Which do you kill? The dog? Or the man?"

She thought a moment. "That would depend on the dog," she said. "If it was one of those smarmy little lapdogs? I'd plug the pooch!" She laughed.

Her blind date smiled. He carefully set his wine glass on the table. "Seriously, though. Which would you shoot?"

She sipped from her glass, held it close. "Well, then. I wouldn't shoot either one. I would . . . abstain. That's it! I would abstain."

"But you *have* to shoot one." He leaned forward. "That's the scenario. You have the gun. One of them has to die."

"I see," she said. *Here we go*, she thought. *The fork in the road. The diverging path.* She looked out the alcove window. Moths pitched madly at the lanterns outside.

"In that case," she said, "if we have an animal and a human being, I would have to shoot the animal. That's the only choice, really." She turned to him. "Isn't it?"

He was still smiling, but blinking rapidly. "This man is a killer. He'll kill again. He has *vowed* to kill again." Her blind date leveled a finger at her. "You have to stop him from killing again."

She shook her head. "I know, but I can't point a gun at a human being and shoot him. I just can't do it." She brightened. "Say, we're both in this scenario, aren't we? Why don't I hand the gun to you?" She batted her eyes. "You'd kill him for me, wouldn't you?"

His smile widened for one second and settled into a thin line.

"Alright," he said, shifting in his chair. "What's your favorite breed of dog?"

She hesitated. She had no favorite breed. She didn't like dogs, and she was about to tell him this when he snapped his fingers.

"Favorite breed," he said. "Come on, come on."

She selected a breed at random.

"OK," he said. "OK." He cleared a spot on the table. Near the wine bottle, a golden Lab pup mewled adorably, gnawing on a bedroom slipper. Slouched against the candlestick, a man watched indifferently. He was, of course, a child killer, slack-jawed and cruel, with cracked lips and stains on his pants and evil in his black, greasy heart. He was the Last Child Killer. Shoot him and all children would be safe, but let him live and he would somehow breed and multiply. Shoot the dog and beloved Labs everywhere would vanish, never to return. Her blind date elaborated on the dire hypothetical consequences, his hands slicing the air, disturbing the candle flame. A fat moth thudded against the window glass next to his head. She watched the moth, the guttering flame, the sheen of flop-sweat on her blind date's forehead.

And then, dessert arrived.

It was the house specialty. They called it Cuore Inverno—a ball of hazelnut gelato inside a dark chocolate shell, drizzled with syrup of pomegranate and positioned within an immense cut-glass goblet dolloped with crème fraîche and dotted with champagne grapes. This was why she had suggested meeting at this café. She picked up her spoon and leaned forward. The man across from her had fallen silent. "Of course, it's just a game," he was saying now. "No biggie."

"Right," she said, gazing into the goblet before her. She gave the ball a sharp whack with the flat of her spoon. Ice cream oozed sweetly from the wound. She pried into it.

"It's just interesting," he was saying. "What people would do, I mean."

She put the spoon into her mouth, sucked on it, and swallowed. She closed her eyes and groaned: "Oh. My. God." They had figured out a way to keep the gelato cold and soft while encasing it in hard chocolate. She'd been hungry all week, coming off the stomach flu. She had starved herself all day, looking forward to this evening, and it was worth it.

The man across from her touched his spoon on the table, then left it alone. "Well," he said. He looked around the café, then back at her. "This was nice," he said. "Wasn't it?" She didn't answer. He watched his blind date work intently on the dessert, watched her finish it, chattering all the while about their dinner together, speaking of it in the past tense, as if this evening had already entered their common memory, as if it had become the story they would tell their friends—the story that he imagined they would both look back upon and laugh about, years from now.

Photo Copyright © Tom Collicott.

David Shields's most recent book, *Reality Hunger: A Manifesto*, was published by Knopf in early 2010. His previous book, *The Thing About Life Is That One Day You'll Be Dead*, was a *New York Times* bestseller. He is the author of eight other books, including *Black Planet: Facing Race During an NBA Season*, a finalist for the National Book Critics Circle Award; *Remote: Reflections on Life in the Shadow of Celebrity*, winner of the PEN/Revson Award; and *Dead Languages: A Novel*, winner of the PEN Syndicated Fiction Award. His essays and stories have appeared in the *New York Times Magazine*, *Harper's*, *Yale Review*, *Village Voice*, *Salon*, *Slate*, *McSweeney's*, and *Utne Reader*; he's written reviews for the *New York Times Book Review*, *Los Angeles Times Book Review*, *Boston Globe*, and *Philadelphia Inquirer*.

David read his essay, *3 Sugar Solutions*, at the 2002 event themed "Midnight Snack."

3 SUGAR SOLUTIONS

Laurie has made chocolate chip cookies, and all night and into the morning I can't stop eating them. "Life isn't good enough for no cigarette," Leonard Michaels once wrote; this is precisely how I've come to view my relationship to sugar. Today was a disaster, I tell myself at least twice a week, stopping in at a cafe that makes the most perfect Rice Krispies Treats, but this tastes delicious. "Eat dessert first," as the bumper sticker says, "life is uncertain." Quentin Tarantino, asked why he eats Cap'n Crunch, replied, "Because it tastes good and is easy to make." Cap'n Crunch, Rice Krispies Treats: I'm addicted to refined sugar in its less refined forms: breakfast cereal, cookies, ice cream, root beer, licorice, peanut brittle, et al., ad nauseam—kid stuff. When I'm happy, I consume sweets to celebrate. When I'm upset, I eat treats as consolation. I'm therefore never without a reason to be in the throes of sugar shock. I don't drink. I don't smoke. I don't do drugs. I do sugar—in massive doses. So what? Who doesn't? What's the harm? Where's the interest? Due to my stutter, much of the glory of sugar is the way it seems like succor to my tired mouth muscles; to me, sugar consumption is a gorgeous allegory about intractable reality and very temporary transcendence.

* * *

On a visit to Los Angeles, I'm sampling two new flavors at the Brentwood Haagen-Dazs when—near midnight—in walks O.J. Simpson with two very young guys in excellent shape. Seniors, say, on the USC football team; I don't know. O.J. is not in excellent shape, not even in good shape, not even close. He's no longer a senior on the USC football team. The air conditioning is on.

I've liked O.J. since I was a kid, because my cousin, a UCLA grad, has always rooted, in a gloating, ungracious manner, against USC. None of us say anything now to O.J. There is shyness to our behavior, but there is also a smidgen of self-respect. There are maybe six or eight people in the store other than me and O.J. and his friends. Part of the tension is the sheer surprise of seeing O.J. ordering ice cream; I've never thought of him doing something so mundane and unhealthy. In a curious way, he is unwelcome or at the very least not wholly embraced; he is intruding a little, maybe, by participating in our slovenliness.

Gallantly (so I first think), O.J. seeks to purchase a woman's ice cream for her. She suddenly looks much prettier to me than she had before. O.J. winks at the two seniors on the USC football team, applies pressure to the crook of the woman's arm, recommends triple brownie overload. I remember thinking, very specifically, O.J.'s kinda tarnishing his reputation here; this was years before he took the Bronco out for a spin on I-5.

The woman smiles a smile that goes exactly so far and no farther, then says, "Thank you but no," looking at me, trying to get me in on this. But I can't. I don't. Suddenly I'm just standing there.

O.J. persists, reiterating his desire to buy an ice cream cone for her. It's like watching a famous suicidal accordion fold in on itself: O.J. keeps nudging the woman up to the counter while she, impressively, impassively, keeps saying, over, and over, "No, thanks, O.J. That won't be necessary. I haven't quite decided yet."

Finally, when O.J. refuses to relent, she points at me and says, "My boyfriend's treating."

"Your boyfriend?" one of O.J.'s minions mutters, in O.J.'s defense. "That man's your boyfriend?"

* * *

My sophomore year of high school my acne problem reached such catastrophic proportions that once a month I drove an hour each way to receive liquid nitrogen treatments from a superserious dermatologist in South San Francisco. His office was catty-corner to a shopping center that housed a Long's drugstore, where I would always first give my prescription for that month's miracle drug to the pharmacist. Then, while I was waiting for the prescription to be filled, I'd go buy a giant bag of Switzer's red licorice. Not the cheap cherry version so much in favor now, though. The darker stuff: claret-colored. I'd tear open the bag, and even if—especially if—my face was still bleeding slightly from all the violence that had just been done to it, I'd start gobbling the licorice while standing in line for the cashier. This may sound a little gooey, but, looking back, I'm hard-pressed now to see the licorice as anything other than some sort of Communion wafer, as if, by swallowing them, my juicy red pimples might become sweet and tasty. I'd absorb them; I'd be absolved. The purity of the contradiction I remember as a kind of ecstasy.

My senior yearbook photo was so airbrushed that people asked me, literally, who it was.

Well, time heals all wounds; so they say. This isn't even remotely true. Time passes, they say. This is true. Ten, twelve, fifteen years passed:

Late one night I crave a bag of claret-colored licorice and the next day I can't find one anywhere, so I write to Switzer's, in St. Louis: whither the good licorice of yesteryear? "Per your inquiry," Bart Kercher, Quality Control Manager, writes back, "our St. Louis facility produces Switzer's licorice candy, Switzer's red candy, Good & Plenty candy, and Good 'n Fruity candy. The 'claret-colored' Switzer's candy which you speak of was produced by a 'batch' cooking operation. Our plant has been modernized and we currently have a continuous cooking system for greater candy uniformity."

A couple of weeks later, a large envelope arrives, bearing Switzer's largesse—licorice whips, strips, bits, Good & Plenty. I rip open the bags and boxes and chew and chew.

Tess Gallagher, a poet, essayist, storywriter, screenwriter and translator was born in 1943 in Port Angeles, Washington. Her first collection of poems, *Instructions to the Double*, won the 1976 Elliston Book Award for "best book of poetry published by a small press." In 1992 she published *Moon Crossing Bridge*, written after the death in 1988 of her husband, internationally recognized master of the short story, Raymond Carver. Other collections include *Dear Ghosts* (Graywolf Press, 2006), *My Black Horse: New and Selected Poems* (1995), and *Owl-Spirit Dwelling* (1994). Her short story collection *The Man from Kinvara* (2009) collects the best of two volumes of stories. Her forthcoming *New and Selected Poems: Midnight Lantern* will be out Fall 2011 from Graywolf. She appears with Robert Altman and others in the DVD *Luck, Trust and Katsup* about the making of the film *Short Cuts*.

Her honors include a fellowship from the Guggenheim Foundation and two National Endowment for the Arts Awards.

Tess wrote the story, *The Why is Missing*, for the inaugural 1999 Bedtime Stories event.

THE WHY IS MISSING

The Why is missing from Why-I-Write—is beside even the missing point of introducing *whys*, one or many, into the doing of something so *inside* the question, so interior to itself.

The truth may be that Why is not a ladder, nor even a footstool to Why-I-write. If I take Why away, I still write, still would ever and always have written, and still don't know Why the slow gaze and supple form of the black horse under the walnut trees ripples through me like river-water when I think toward it.

If Why was my captain, I was missing from my platoon. While others have had their Whys strapped to their shoulders like canteens, or rifles at the ready, I have been AWOL from Why for the entire campaign.

Those who have been certain of Why they did what they did, could mean business: could vanquish, have causes, find targets, take aim! They could perform both the stationary and the moving miracle of targets. But where was my Why?—none had been issued! I could never point to or surround or hoist the flag of any reason for what I was doing, as I was doing it, as—body and invisible soul—I kept myself to the task and joy of writing.

I was, after all, writing as if it were as necessary as breathing. Why breathing? Because, in my case, to write is like taking in oxygen for the invisible backpack of the soul. In truth, I can never tell when the mountain of a moment will spire up under me and require more than the normal amount of such oxygen.

At the Cantina of Unwordly Worlds when they ask me: what will you have? I always say "Oxygen, please," and then I ask for a fresh napkin and begin to write on it. At some roadside cantinas I hear oxygen is trucked in across bridges, all named "Why" to rhyme with the movie "The Bridge Over the River Kwai" or after someone like D.B. Cooper, who tumbled from the sky and who will always, like the bones of the Why, be missing in the forest somewhere in the wild Pacific Northwest.

It is important, in fact, that Why *be* missing, like the body of a saponified woman in my childhood lake, Lake Crescent. This woman eventually did float to the surface so her murderer could be caught—her Why so entangled by then in his, that even when she floated up, there was no choice for her, since any *dead*, however you get there, is finally beyond choice or reason. But my *Why* refuses to float up. It constantly effaces its reasons, possibly to preserve its ultimate freedom from utility.

The Secretary-of-Souls is also mistaken to ask for my topic sentence, so she will know why I'm writing what is mysteriously appearing in invisible plain sight, as it spins across pages, despite the orphanhood of my two-legged understanding of the spider: Why. More oxygen, please! My spider can't spin without the word-stuff she is making, seemingly out of nothing. And she has to spin. But that isn't her Why or her Whinny or her Whither-thou-goest. Anything you *have-to* can't be a Why.

Consider again Lake Crescent and all the mishaps and myths associated with it. Take, for instance, the children whose bus took a bad turn and pollinated the lake with all those dead futures. Just children. Innocent of the bad turn. Missing from a life now of topic sentences telling everyone what they were going to grow up to be, or do, for the rest of their never-to-be-lives...

So I am at the Cantina, writing on my napkin what the dead children might say about the missing-ness of their lives, not to mention their ever-grieving parents who will miss them for reasons of blood and beyond—no, the parents can never be consoled. With that in mind, I decide to write instead for the gravediggers. After the recovery of some of the bodies, these gravediggers were interviewed about the drowned children for whom they had dug graves. They wept uncontrollably for those children, children they didn't know. Why did they weep? Maybe the alchemy of dead-children briefly transforms death, so dead-children are not children after all; but tears migrating back to our faces, as if we too, for long moments, went missing when any child died.

I bend to my napkin. Forty years, in and out of the Cantina, writing out of the very center of The Don't-Know-Why, staring down the death-glance of a daisy.

There is a loud commotion and I look up. Captain Why has sauntered into the Cantina with a half dozen raw recruits. They seem a little glazed-over and their bayonets are glistening so I almost want to put down my pen and let myself be conscripted— they are that compelling in their straight-ahead candor about the sacking of several villages that morning. *"It had to be done,"* Captain Why is now detailing to the waitress. She has a look of disbelief on her cherub face. Her name is Maggie-May and she glances nervously at me, hunched over my napkin. She knows at this moment I am probably in the wrong place at the wrong time.

Once she has served the Captain and his minions from the menu she comes over and casually leans on the counter with her beautiful head cupped in her palms, and says, "Why don't you buy some regular paper?"

"I like the way the napkin tears when I press too hard," I tell her. I don't say that it is also important to run out of room while writing, and to have to involve a bystander like her by asking for yet another insufficient napkin. Nor do I mention the gravediggers—how I need them, need how they don't know Why they are weeping for the children who don't belong to them and who they will never know.

I want to blurt out to Captain Why who's eating his buffalo burger: "What about the feeling of tears falling when you don't know Why?" But just then the napkin tears, and my pen leaves a murderous little black hyphen on the formica counter—

* * *

"That Captain," Maggie-May confides, the next time I'm in, "he was shouting after you left: 'Why Why Why!' and pointing to your hyphen." (She has a low opinion of the captain because he only eats the yolks of his eggs.)

So she looks after me as usual, lets me serve up my own oxygen with a fresh napkin or two, and generally lets me be, because what I want isn't on the menu. But that's no reason not to keep her customers happy, here at the Cantina of Unworldly

Worlds. After all, I am a regular. I enjoy the elegant, unspoken ease of coming and going as someone known, if not expected. I careen on my swivel chair at the counter while my hand races along behind the pen, tattering words into the napkin, which— like a sacred papyrus made of butterfly wings—reminds me of the fragility of the very enterprise of trying to articulate, as I consider, as I write, as I—

Sky House
September 11, 1998

Photo Copyright © David Cooper.

Pulitzer Prize-winning playwright August Wilson is one of the most influential writers in American theater. He is best known for his unprecedented cycle of 10 plays, often called the Pittsburgh Cycle because all but one play is set in Pittsburgh's Hill District neighborhood where he grew up. Self-educated at the local Carnegie library after dropping out of school at age 15, Wilson began to write poetry in 1965. Drawn to the theater and inspired by the civil rights movement, in 1968 August Wilson co-founded the Black Horizons Theatre in the Hill District of Pittsburgh. His third play, "Ma Rainey's Black Bottom" (1982) won Wilson wide recognition as a dramatist and interpreter of the African American experience. August has been honored with numerous awards, including two Tony Awards and two Pulitzer Prizes for drama.

August, a three-time Bedtime Stories contributor, read his story *How Hilda Grovenshire Ate Her Way to Fame* at the 2002 event themed "Midnight Snack." August passed away in 2005 and we at Humanities Washington, as do countless others, miss him tremendously.

HOW HILDA GROVENSHIRE
ATE HER WAY TO FAME

Ihave throughout the years been known to be dogged in my pursuits, not the least of which was Constanza Romero, as I was want to have a wife of great beauty, vivid intelligence and splendid virtue, given to singing over the pots in the kitchen, and who might one day give me a daughter who would share these attributes, and like her mother, ripen with each dawn. I have been equally dogged and undaunted in my pursuit of the truth behind the fairy tales and stories that we so innocently and thoughtlessly tell our children. In this guise I have rankled many a good parent who have accused me of upsetting the apple-cart, of rousing sleeping dogs, and I have, I am happy to report, earned their ire, though I hasten to disclaim the accusation that I pummel old ladies with my umbrella. I have been, as my fortune is good, blessed with a daughter to whom I did dutifully tell, in the customary versions, the fairy tales that have visited us all in our childhood. But I dare say I shall not leave it at that. As she grows older and acquires a greater understanding of the vicissitudes of life I will share with her my discoveries of the lessons contained therein.

My recent travels led me to Berlin and as is my habit, I browsed the used book stalls, searched in the attics of farmhouses, the basements of cathedrals, and on Gorlitz Street, near the end just before it turns into Kowary, a bookseller pressed into my hands, for all of two dollars, a small notebook in which the following was written. I present it, without comment, for the reader's inspection.

CONCERNING THE EVENTS OF THE YEARS OF THE FAMINE.

Now as I write this in my ninety-sixth year my muscles have stiffened and my joints have weakened so as to make even a visit to my favorite chair in the garden a laborious task I seldom undertake anymore. However, while my body has suffered the natural inducements of old age, my mind is unimpeachable in its recall, especially regarding the events of the years of the famine and my dear, dear sister Gretel whose perpetual rest I attend with yearly visits to the small graveyard where she is buried. Of her I will always have the fondest memories. Unbeknownst to many, I also visit the grave where the bones of Hilda Grovenshire are interred as an act of contrition that always ends with my damning her inconsiderate and insulting ideas of culinary delight.

Our dear mother died in the first year of the famine. She was a generous woman unswerving in her devotion, and both Gretel and I were at a loss and hourly grieved her. Our father drowned his grief in the arms of the local seamstress whom he married. It was a union that both Gretel and I regretted as we thought it unfortunate that our father would fall prey to the fat thighs of such a selfish and manipulative woman. One day as she spent an inordinate amount of time lingering over the empty pots, our father was able to perceive her devilish and carnivorous designs. Dark rumors of the villagers succumbing to unspeakable acts laid uneasy on his mind and he packed the last morsels of bread and ferreted Gretel and I out of the house and into the dark German forest with its many wolves and huntsmen.

We used the bread he had given us to mark our passage back to the house as we resolved to rescue our father from what we perceived to be his sure fate. It was not a very intelligent plan as the birds devoured the crumbs leaving us lost and wandering ever deeper into the forest and away from the only home we had ever known. You must know it was a frightful and uncertain time for us, the details of which I need not go into here. Only know that we resolved that whatever happened, whatever our fate, we would share it together, and that our devotion to each other could never be challenged or torn asunder.

On the third day after a particularly harried night during which we were surrounded by wolves baying among themselves like priests, we suddenly came to a clearing and there, before our very eyes, as if in a dream, was a house made of gingerbread. It was a sight, the memory of which I shall never forget, for by it we were rescued, our prayers had been answered and we were given a reprieve from a sure and certain fate that our severe hunger forebode. The gods, dear reader, can be cruel beyond what St. Augustine in his famous Confessional called, "faultless cruelty." The house, we discovered, was made of tree bark and cleverly disguised to look like gingerbread. It was the abode of one, Hilda Grovenshire. She smiled when she saw us and her kindly demeanor put us at ease. She invited us inside and served us each a large bowl of stew. We were soon to discover that her generosity was a mask to aid her devilish nature. In the corner of the second room were two cages, odd not only in their construction, but we were puzzled as to the reason for their existence. Certainly we had never encountered such in any of the houses we had ever visited.

One the second day of our stay, Hilda Grovenshire tricked me into one of the cages on the pretense of having me repair it, and slammed and locked the door behind me. Gretel screamed and Hilda slapped her hard across the face and cackled a stream of vile and obscene abuse. My heart went out for poor Gretel as this sudden reversal sent her into a state of shock that I was later scarcely able to pull her from. Hilda Grovenshire was more wicked than we could imagine, having only the experience of our stepmother, who now appeared saintly, to measure it against. She sent Gretel scurrying about on a relentless round of chores which, while exhausting, gave her free run of the house. At night, she was locked in the cage beside me.

One day as she was tending to the vegetable garden where Hilda grew turnips and green beans, Gretel discovered a row of cages, seven in all, along a corridor at the rear of the house. To our dismay we learned that Hans Berber, the kind old shoemaker who was always quick with a smile and a piece of candy, was an occupant of one of the cages. His wife, a fat, jolly woman of indeterminate age, had until recently occupied the cage next to him. One morning when he had awoken she was gone and he had not seen or heard from her since. I need not tell you that Gretel and I did not eat our ration of stew that night and had difficulty keeping it down the days following. But eat we must if we were to survive and in time we came to consider ourselves fortunate.

Occasionally visitors came to visit Hilda and would sit in the kitchen where she would serve them tea and thin slices of black bread. We could overhear their conversation and their reports of the famine spreading sank our morale. We learned that the visitors were part of a witches coven and their visits were an exchange of bounty and recipes. Usually after these visits our diet improved. Once a few carrots were added to the stew and tasted strongly of black pepper, which was famously scarce throughout the whole country.

One night as Gretel returned to the cages she whispered that she had managed to smuggle the witch's diary and in the still of the night, by the light of the moon, we read the details of our capture, and with a shuddering grief that gnawed at our stomachs, the fate of Hans Berber's wife. What we read next horrified us. Seven words detailing Hilda Grovenshire's plan for Gretel and me.

Dear readers you must understand that we were not unintelligent and knew long before our capture of the sacrifices that were being made to subdue the horrible famine. Gretel and I were all too ready, if we must, to make the ultimate sacrifice as so many of our brethren had. Although it was spoken in rumors, we knew as everyone did that such unspeakable acts were real and that they would pass judgment of our dear Lord and Savior for they bore no moral laxity, but rather the urge to life and fulfillment was a duty understood by all and the unfortunate souls whose lot called for sacrifice approached their calling as an act of charity. Gretel and I had long discussions and resolved were we so chosen, that thoughtful prayer would be our only solace and that we would pronounce it without rebuke. In our resolution we had found strength and continued to persevere. But this! These seven words! This was outrageous! We would not stand for it. No, we would, on our honor and self-respect, revolt. And so we made our plans.

The locks to the cages were made of wood and had been fashioned, we later learned, by Guntar Holfsbrun, the locksmith from the nearby village of Lurlen, a slovenly man whose reputation for strong drink had cost him a Royal appointment. The locks were of ingenious design but poorly executed as Gunter's drinking blunted his genius. With some difficulty I managed to free myself. I had less difficulty with Gretel's lock and we tiptoed toward the back of the house with the idea of freeing Hans Berber and making our way, with Han's sure knowledge, to the nearest village. Needless to say, as Hilda Grovenshire was a witch, her familiar was a large black cat, who upon seeing Gretel and I sneaking toward the rear of the house, sent up an ungodly wail as deafening as any new born baby's cry. We were caught. Hilda's sense of propriety, her sense of security and her sense of outrage were all violated and a more fearsome and hideous visage I cannot imagine. For a brief second we were stunned. With the cat shrieking in the background and Hilda approaching us, trembling with rage at our audacity, I recovered my senses and as a means of protecting myself, I struck her a blow that landed at her temple. She wobbled about with a strange look on her face, then fell. Gretel and I were surprised when she did not move. We released Hans from the cage and together we plotted our next move. We must notify the authorities, of course. We would explain everything. It was all so easy to understand, or so we thought, and perhaps it would have been, had not winter set in at a sudden.

At my trial, I admitted that in truth I did strike her. Yes. But it was a blow for our freedom. I had no way of knowing that the snow would make the forest impenetrable until the spring thaw. On the surface it would seem, as it did to the authorities, that I killed her to ensure our survival in those most trying of times. Hans Berber testified to the truth but they dismissed him as an old man gone soft in the head and his testimony went unheeded. Our stepmother testified falsely and maliciously that we were hired out to Hilda Grovenshire for the year and that Hilda was known to be a kind and gentle woman. Our dear father was unable to offer the truth as the famine consumed him during the long Winter that Gretel and I and Hans Berber spent trapped in that damnable witch's cottage, the only consolation of which, we did find, no doubt part of the Coven's shared exchange, small packets of spices, which made our various stews and soups not only edible but, I am almost ashamed to say, delectable as well.

It was during the seventh year of my incarceration that an old woodsman, together with his wife, seeking an idyllic respite from the burly confusion of life with its sundry and unpredictable happenings that bulk at orchestration, purchased the cottage and discovered human bones buried in the corner of the small vegetable garden. If I neglected to say that Hilda Grovenshire had been married four times and that each of her husbands had, according to rumor, abandoned her, engendering great sympathy from the local villages, it was not hitherto important to my story.

Further investigation revealed the dreadful truth of the matter and uncovered the witch's coven, several members of which confessed to their dietary practices and were burned at the stake. Hilda Grovenshire became famous as The Cannibal Witch of Gruenfeld Forest and I as the Instrument of Poetic Justice. For years I received a steady stream of visitors making inquiries and presenting me with small tokens of appreciation for the comfort it gave them to know that God was in his Heaven, and he would, sometimes through mysterious and unknowable means, make everything right. Gradually the visits came to a halt and I went on with my life and thought the matter forgotten until this morning when the brothers Jacob and Wilheim Grimm came to satisfy their intrigue. I related to them the story and thought to write it down while it is still fresh in my mind. Though I have long gotten over the matter, I still bristled at the thought of those seven words which inspired Gretel and me to revolt: "The Children will make a delicious midnight snack."

Photo Copyright © Paul Joseph Brown.

Laura Kalpakian has received a National Endowment for the Arts award, a Pushcart Prize, the Pacific Northwest Booksellers Association Award, and the first Anahid Literary Award for an American Writer of Armenian descent. She is the author of ten novels, including *American Cookery,* nominated for the 2007 IMPAC/Dublin Literary Award. Her short fiction has been gathered in three collections, including *Fair Augusto,* which won the PEN/West Award for Best Short Fiction. She is a former trustee of Humanities Washington.

Laura wrote the original *El Rancho Stucco* for the 2002 event themed "Midnight Snack," which inspired her to expand and enhance the story.

EL RANCHO STUCCO

You might miss it, especially at sunset. You might drive right by. You might not notice the tumbleweeds struggling against the chain link fence. You would see the locked gate, and a faded, hand-painted sign hanging, lopsided, the wood pocked with buckshot, *Beware of Dog*. You would hear the wind, and in the distance, barking curs. Beyond the gate, you would see an unpaved road leading to low, rambling buildings, colorless, clustered under dusty bougainvillea, sheltered from view and shaded by towering eucalyptus, sycamores and pepper trees. You'd smell smoke from the washtub fire in the carport. Catch the whiff of stringy meat and peppers grilling. You'd hear the rumble of deep voices, splattered laughter, off-key mariachis playing, and the chickens clucking and quarreling. You'd hear whinnying horses in corrals, the bleating of complacent sheep, and the bells tied to ill-tempered goats who wander the place at will. This is El Rancho Stucco, retirement home of Pancho and the Cisco Kid. El Rancho Stucco—these few pathetic, unkempt acres, ramshackle bunkhouses, barns, a one-story rambler house, carport, tin roofed chicken sheds, abandoned pickups, rusted cars—these are the last remnant of Pancho's family's great wealth.

In nearly two hundred TV episodes, and in B-westerns before that, Pancho was always Cisco's sidekick. *O Pancho! O Ceesco!* Pancho played the sidekick according to formula: scruffy, grinning, a little goofy, ruled by his appetites, that is, hunger, not lust, certainly not lust. In the Golden Age of Television, not even the Cisco Kid could suffer or evince lust. Cisco might chastely kiss a señorita, but Pancho could only say, *O Ceesco, I am so hongry!* Pancho offered comic relief to the Cisco's Kid's bravado and splendor. But in truth, Pancho is the man of bravado and splendor. He is an aristocrat, descended from a distinguished Southern California family possessed of land and power, Mexican grandees who could trace their people back four hundred years.

In Pancho's hacienda childhood, cattle dotted a thousand golden hills. Food was plentiful, entertainments lavish; silvery fountains whispered in courtyards. The horses were all fast, fine specimens descended from Spanish Andalusians. The women were all beautiful and fine cooks. The men were reckless. From these reckless men, little Pancho learned rope tricks, to jump on and off as the horse gallops, and many other feats of derring-do. He called himself the Macho Muchacho. All the women in his family indulged him in this. These lovely women took Pancho into their confidence, their affections, into their kitchens and taught him the secrets of *cocina Mexicana*, taught him to grind spices, guided his hands expertly with the mortar and pestle, showed him the teasing slap that would transform mere cornmeal into fresh tortillas.

Pancho was only a boy that long ago evening—one old century slowly oozing toward another—when his grandfather, presiding proudly at the long, table, extended his hospitality to all, including a soft-spoken *gringo* from Virginia. The meal was excellent, the women languorous, the men attentive, the hibiscus blooming, and no doubt a lone guitar strummed in the distance while the breeze stirred dried oleander blossoms at their feet. A fountain nearby. Your typical evening of lost times.

The Virginian said he had a horse, en route from Virginia to San Francisco by boat. His horse was so fast that the Virginian had named him Death. The Virginian proposed a race between Death and El Cid, Pancho's grandfather's horse, the great, the undefeated Andalusian.

Pancho's grandfather laughed. All his guests laughed. In race after race, year after year, no horse had ever outrun El Cid. That any horse, even Death, could beat the Andalusian? Preposterous! Such an idea was *loco*. They offered the stupid Virginian their veiled condescension and more wine.

The Virginian said the day of the horse was finished anyway, past. He said the future belonged to the motorcar. Again the grandfather and his guests laughed. The motorcar? Smelly. Unreliable. Uncomfortable. Requiring no grace from the rider and offering none. *Loco*. Nothing could compare with the sight of a fine horse, especially an Andalusian, and nothing could be more satisfying or beautiful than to be on horseback. The men, women and children present, all agreed to this.

I'll bet a thousand dollars on Death, said the Virginian, and I'll match all other bets. To the guests' surprise, he withdrew from his black coat, cash. He set the fluttering stack on the table and put a candlestick on top. The candle flickered and dripped. He lit a thin cigar, and added: I'll put my rider on Death. You put whoever you like on El Cid.

Pancho's grandfather took the bet. They set a date some five months hence to give the challenger time to get his horse to California.

After the gringo left, his grandfather clapped the boy, Pancho, on the shoulder, and declared that the little Macho Muchacho would ride the legendary El Cid to glory. The guests all toasted the Macho Muchacho. Then everyone—grandfather, his wife and her relatives, his children and grandchildren and their spouses and relatives, his Mexican grandee ancestors going back four hundred years—laughed themselves silly. Death would have to be ridden from San Francisco all the way to Los Angeles for the race. It was a long ride, rough terrain. The horse would be spavined and winded by the time it got here.

A nine-mile oval racecourse was laid out on a field not far from what is now downtown Los Angeles. Knowing no challenger could beat El Cid, all of Southern California laughed at Death. In the five months between the challenge and the day itself, word of this race percolated, and a betting frenzy ensued, and escalated. Bookies, and bankers and livestock brokers took fat commissions and kept careful records. The poor bet what they could: two bits, a dollar, five maybe, a few head of cattle, the deed to a ten-acre dump in Malibu canyon. The rich relished the opportunity to beat Death and get even richer; they put down land cattle, and gold. Pancho's grandfather, alone, bet $25,000 in gold, 500 mares, 500 heifers, 500 sheep.

The day of the race, all the wagered livestock were penned near the race course, acres and acres of bleating, baying and whinnying, the deep protesting bellowing of the cattle. The animal cacophony was deafening. (Pancho can still hear it in his troubled sleep, his bad dreams, even now when he is a very old man, living at El Rancho Stucco, sleeping alone and beset by *mal sueños.* The noise does not wake him. No, the silence does that, the void.)

The day of the race—the day Death would be beaten—everyone in Southern California, rich and poor, young and old, gathered at the nine-mile track, and milled in the afternoon heat. Humanity, two-dozen deep jostled near the track. Children scrambled to the upper limbs of trees to watch. People stood on chairs in wagons. Grandstands, built at the finish line for the wealthy, swayed with the weight of hundreds. Dust rose up from the feet of thousands. The dust glinted, little gilded motes in the sunshine.

As young Pancho, on the back of El Cid, rode up to the grandstand, they cheered him. El Cid wore a silver-studded saddle. Pancho wore golden leather chaps and a fine sombrero; his mother's blue silk handkerchief waved from his breast pocket. The crowd roared, ¡Macho Muchacho! ¡Macho Muchacho! They threw flowers before him as El Cid pranced to the starting line. Which would also be the finish line. The other horse was not yet there. People joked that Death would forfeit. As always, this thought comforted the living.

Then, from a long way off, there came a coughing sound, a low mechanical gurgle and a small caravan of horseless, motorized vehicles appeared. Three of them. Men wearing bizarre goggles that made them look like flies, with tight caps on their heads, and long white angel-wing coats stepped out of a Welch touring car when it spluttered to a halt. There was another Welch touring car right behind this, and a third car lumbered in the distance. The vehicles were covered with dust, but you could still see the seats were red leather, the fittings were of brass, and the rubber tires had spokes of red painted wood. The last motorcar, also a Welch, was enormous, a six-cylinder, and pulled behind it what looked to be a lightweight freight car with an end-loading door and a small, barred window at the front.

The Virginian removed his goggles and waved to the grandstand. No flowers were thrown at him. His crew opened the end-loading door of the small freight car and brought forth Death. Death was dazzling, white, sleek, strong, so beautifully groomed his white tail and mane were braided and tied with white ribbons. Death wore no silver saddle. The saddle was little more than a blanket thrown over Death's powerful back. He was not spavined at all. He had not been ridden from San Francisco to Los Angeles. He had come in this caravan of sturdy motorized vehicles.

The crowd momentarily hushed. Then, they jeered Death and his rider. They insulted and scoffed and mocked. They especially excoriated Death's rider. Look at him! He was not a local boy like the Macho Muchacho known to all. This rider was a man so small and tensile, so wiry, he might have been an albino frog. Goggles covered his eyes, and a tight white cap covered his head. His hands were covered in white gloves and soft, silky clothing fluttered along his back like the wings of white moths.

At the sound of the starting gun, El Cid bolted into the lead, and left Death in his wake, eating his golden dust. Take that, Death! thought Pancho, spurring El Cid on. As El Cid tore forward, Pancho bent low over the horse, smelling El Cid's equine sweat, and tasting victory. But somewhere, perhaps half way around the course, the unthinkable happened. The challenger swept up alongside El Cid. They stayed neck in neck for a time, and Death's pale rider turned and grinned at Pancho, his face made the more horrible by the goggles. Then the impossible happened: Death charged ahead, and Pancho saw only his flying white hooves. Then, not even hooves. As Pancho was enveloped in Death's white dust, time and distance seemed to swell and bloat, meld and spray and fall away. When at long last, Pancho galloped across that finish line, he crossed into a state, indeed, a country of suspended disbelief. Victorious Death had gathered up all the crowd, all the animals, all the sound and voices, and left only a massive emptiness. Not a leaf or a tumbleweed stirred. Not even the wind. Would Pancho ever recover from the void, the silence?

* * *

His grandfather's reckless betting lost the family's vast wealth, and the cattle that had dotted the hillsides. Eventually, the grandfather lost the hillsides themselves. Finally he was reduced to this worthless scrap, El Rancho Stucco, where he grumbled into old age, a bitter recluse. The whole family suffered; many died of shame, some of simple chagrin. The lovely women dried and hardened like chilis hung from rafters; their penniless daughters could not find husbands, and their sons took up manual labor instead of going to school.

Pancho, however, was not defeated. Resilient, energetic, accomplished on horseback, he kept the name Macho Muchacho. Never mind that he was no longer a boy, but a man, young, handsome with thick, curling hair, a fine moustache and a body both lithe and solid. And, even if he were only indifferently educated, he remained an aristocrat. He loved horses, yes, but he loved opera as well. He went again and again to the new Los Angeles Opera house to see the divine Emma Calvé sing *Carmen*. Inspired by Bizet, by Emma Calvé and *Carmen*, Pancho learned to fight bulls. His augmented his native skills and instincts with disciplined training. He anticipated his debut in the ring.

In those days the bull ring was just that, a solid ring with bleachers and a ticket booth. Lots of small businesses and homes with chickens clustered nearby, and even after bullfighting vanished, the community remained. The place became known as Chavez Ravine. Dodger Stadium now rises on the ghosts of Chavez Ravine, which itself rested on obliterated ¡olés!, and the dried blood of animals.

That day, Pancho's bull would be the very last contest. The bullfighters before him had already proven themselves *muy hombre*. To resounding ¡olés! they had slain many bulls. The vanquished bulls were pulled from the arena and slaughtered on the spot.

The crowd was happy, enthusiastic, their hungers sharpened because everyone knew that soon, at the little stands and cantinas just outside the bull ring, there would be fresh tacos. Really fresh.

At last the Macho Muchacho, with Bizet's immortal music ringing in his ears, stepped into the ring, flourished his red cape, bowed to the surrounding throngs. Astonishingly, the crowd jeered him, hooted at the Macho Muchacho! Many remembered El Cid, remembered his grandfather's arrogance, and their lost fortunes, large or small. The people heaped abuse on Pancho and his family. Against this derision, Pancho had only his pride, his *muy hombre* strength and beauty. He stood erect and flourished his red cape, gave the nod that the bull should be released. But this bull did not thunder into the ring to take part in this ancient dance of skill and valor. No. This bull did not even charge. This bull, too, scoffed at Pancho. Yes. Unthinkable, but yes. And then, from unthinkable to impossible: the bull flicked his tail, and walked away from Pancho. Trotted, actually.

Hilarious laughter erupted from the crowd, and rippled all through the bleachers. The bull snorted, pranced triumphantly, and executed, a bullish bow for which the women cast flowers at the animal, and insults at Pancho, who stood unmoving in the ring. Soon, their humor having worn thin, the crowds booed Pancho one last time, and left for the tacos which were ready nearby.

Alone with the bull and desperate to prove himself the Macho Muchacho, Pancho taunted the bull repeatedly, called him names in Spanish and cast aspersions on his female relatives. The bull snorted and lay down.

¡You stupid bull! cried Pancho, ¡Fight me!.

The bull said he was through with that. Look what it had got the others.

¡What! Pancho whispered, astounded. ¿A Talking Bull?

Be reasonable, said the Talking Bull. Kill me and you eat for a week. Keep me and I can be useful. I can tell fortunes. I can see the future.

So Pancho took the Talking Bull home to El Rancho Stucco.

His grandfather spluttered rage, and said: ¿How can you bring that bull here? Kill him. We will eat for a week.

Pancho said: You made your bets. I'm making mine. I'm betting on this Talking Bull. He can tell the future.

The grandfather walked away, swearing in Spanish.

To the bull, Pancho said: Now, talk or be tacoed.

The bull told him the most incredible story! The fortune-telling bull prophesied that Pancho would become famous! A legend in films!

¿Films? asked Pancho. ¿You mean those silly one-reelers clicking and clacking, casting flickering images on walls hung with bedsheets?

Listen up—the Talking Bull foretold—films would not always be one-reelers. Films would not be shown in small, close rooms where people sat on benches, smoked and spat while the picture was projected on to a bedsheet hung from the wall. Films would not require a spinster to play the piano. No, the bull declared, one day films would have voices and full orchestras; they would be two-hour extravaganzas and employ millions of people in thousands of capacities whose names would unroll for hours at the end of every picture; they would dazzle audiences with CG technology and cost hundreds of millions of dollars.

Pancho could not wrap his mind around the notion of hundreds of millions or CG technology, but when the bull said that one day films would be shown in palaces, grand as the Opera House, grander, that he understood. He did not believe it, but he understood. The bull said popcorn would come in buckets the size of troughs, and the theatres would be air-conditioned.

¿What's air conditioned? ¿What's popcorn?

Don't interrupt, said the bull, going on: Pancho, you must leave here at once, and apply to be an actor.

Pancho spat and sneered: ¿An actor? ¡I am the Macho Muchacho!

The Talking Bull let that pass in silence.

When he spoke again, the bull foretold Pancho's future: As an actor Pancho's fame would grow slowly. Beginning with bit parts using his horsemanship, his trick riding, and feats of derring-do, Pancho would play Bad Guys, and learn to growl and look dangerous, really mean Bad Guys with names like *Rodrigo* and *Chico*, and *Jose Gomez*. And he would play really foolish roles like *Dr. Zodiac Z. Zippe* and *Tobias Chump*. Difficult for an aristocrat, a proud man, but—the bull snorted through the ring in his nose—

face it, the days of the grandees are over. Look around you. El Rancho Stucco, he scoffed.

Pancho let that pass in silence.

As an actor, you will be loved. You will be rich. You will have a mansion and three wives and five *muchachos*.

Yes, said Pancho, Women love me.

It will not happen as you expect. You will not be famous for your way with women.

The turning point of Pancho's acting career, the bull prophesied, would come in 1936 working on a film called *Moonlight Murders* where Pancho would meet another bit player, a Romanian actor. The Roumanian—though very handsome, black hair, a high nose, beautiful teeth—he too had been stuck films like *Pals of the Prairie* and cast as characters with names like *Chihuahua Ramirez*. He and Pancho would become best friends. But then, in a 1945 film, the Roumanian would be offered the title role in *The Cisco Kid*, a B-Western, mere Saturday matinee fare. The Roumanian would suggest Pancho for the supporting role . The Roumanian would *become* the Cisco Kid. He would put on silver-studded chaps, and the silver-banded sombrero, and a silver saddle. Pancho would wear a calico bandana and a straw sombrero. Pancho would remain his faithful Sidekick.

¿What is a side kick? asked Pancho. It sounds painful.

Sidekick. One word, said the bull. You will be the Dean of American Sidekicks.

¿What's the Dean?

You ask too many questions. I'm not a Rand-McNally to the future.

¿What's a Rand-McNally?

Shut up and listen. In a voice worthy of Moses, the Talking Bull foretold that after many B-Western adventures, *The Cisco Kid* would move to television, half-hour episodes, in the Golden Age of Television.

¿What's television? Asked the Macho Muchacho, unable to stop himself.

Television will take you into the homes and hearts of little *muchachos* and buckaroos everywhere. They will wave to you and call your name down Colorado Boulevard. You will ride in every Tournament of Roses Parade. You will be the Grand Marshall. You will throw candy to the children, and kisses to the beautiful girls on floats, princesses, every one of them.

¡I like this! ¡Tell me more!

You tax me. My powers are spent and I am tired. You must never sell El Rancho Stucco. You will need it. And one last word of caution: watch out for the Red Rock. Now, lead me to the cows and clover.

* * *

During the Golden Age of Television, and in bringing justice to the Old West, the Cisco Kid never struggled with guilt, or nuanced decisions. His courage was never in question. He never killed anyone. He hardly ever sweated. Basically, he just stepped into the sunshine, caught the light on his silver-studded chaps and blinded the villains. Bad Guys were always put behind bars, flung into pasteboard hoosegows. At the end of every half hour episode the señoritas were always grateful to Cisco; they pressed their lips to his cheek in farewell, since Pancho and Cisco never stayed in the towns where they had vanquished evil and restored order. After accepting the gratitude of the stupid locals (usually *gringos* who could not defend themselves) Cisco and Pancho said *adiós*. Cisco mounted his horse, Diablo. Pancho got on Loco. (Yes, he named his horse Loco to remind himself always of the gringo who was not *loco*, of the horse Death, and his pale rider streaking past.) But before they left town, and galloped westward toward next week's adventure, Pancho always said: *O Ceesco*. And Ceesco said: *O Pancho*.

Times were good, even great. Everyone worked all year round, year after year. The series was successful, unchanging, and everyone had steady paychecks, hot coffee on set, cold beers after the shoot, and lots of laughs on location. Cisco and Pancho were best amigos, and everyone got along just fine: Cisco, Pancho, the Bad Guys who needed to be vanquished, the starlet-señoritas who needed to be kissed and saved, or saved and kissed. Mischievous Pancho played pranks on the starlets who laughed, and chided him. The same stuntmen worked year after year, the same wardrobe girls, the same cameramen, and mariachis who played at faked fiestas and faux cantinas, the wranglers who hauled the horses to and from the locations, the chumps who wrote the scripts, the sound man who shook the thunder rolls, the producers who stood around and smoked, the directors who yelled *Action* and *Cut*. *The Cisco Kid* went on and on and on.

But inevitably, over the years, jealousies arose. Pancho's prowess on horseback seemed to Cisco an insult. He declared on the set that he, Cisco, should have the most daring feats. After all, Pancho was the not-so-smart sidekick. The producers pointed out that Pancho could do his own stunts and Cisco could not. Why hire a stuntman for Cisco when Pancho could ride like that for free? Cisco declared he would do his own stunts.

Pancho laughed out loud: You are a Roumanian, what do you know of riding and roping and jumping on and off your horse? Leave these things to the experts, to men who have grown up in the saddle and with cattle on a thousand hills.

But the Cisco Kid insisted. After all, he wore a silver-spangled sombrero. Pancho wore a bandana and a big grin.

The producers stood firm, and Pancho felt vindicated. Thereafter, to prove himself more *muy hombre* than Cisco, Pancho performed stunts not even called for in the script; week by week, his derring-do became more breathtaking. But his friendship with the Roumanian strained to the breaking point, their quarrel festered, their estrangement complete. They ceased to speak unless the camera rolled.

At last, one of the writers wrote an episode where the Sidekick saved the Hero. Here was Pancho's long-sought opportunity to do more than grin and say, *O Ceesco, I am so hongry*. Pancho sent the writer of this episode two dozen tamales, hand-made by his third wife, and a bottle of the best tequila from Rosie's Cantina. Cisco did not like this story, but the producers softened him up, saying it was only one episode, after all.

The climactic scene would play thus: Pancho would draw the fire of some Bad Guys while Cisco went round to surprise them from behind. Then a Bad Guy, unseen by Cisco, would push a fake rock down an incline. This rock would hit Cisco who would then sprawl as though knocked unconscious, and just as the Bad Guys were about to kill Cisco, Pancho would dash to his rescue. He would hold all four Bad Guys at gun point, make them tie each other up while he ministered to Cisco who would be on the ground, eyes closed, powerless until roused by his faithful Sidekick.

This scene was the last shot of the working day. It was 100 degrees. The nearest cold beer was miles from this remote desert location. They rehearsed once, everything except the final segment. If they pushed the fake rock downhill for rehearsal, they would just have to push it back up for the filming. That would take time.

The director told everyone to take their places. Pancho, seated on Loco, clicked his pistol prop, ready to spring into action and rescue Cisco. The clapper called out *Battle of Red Rock Pass, Scene 12, Take One,* Pancho gasped, a sharp stab of anxiety, fiery, intense as heartburn. *Red Rock?*

...Wasn't he supposed to...

Action!

Cisco, at the bottom of the arroyo, stalked the Bad Guys from behind. *Hands Up!* Cisco commanded. But wait! The camera pointed at the Bad Guy poised on a cliff above! The Bad Guy pushed the big fake boulder downhill.

The boulder was fake, but it also had girth, weight and momentum; the hill was actually very steep, and the laws of gravity kicked in as the boulder bounded down, accelerating, and hit Cisco directly on the top of his silver sombrero. As the script instructed, Cisco fell, sprawled, splayed in an ungainly position, and the camera rolled on.

Pancho rode up, rope swirling, six-gun blazing, and just as Bad Guys aimed their guns at the hapless, prone Cisco, Pancho jumped off Loco, and ordered all the Bad Guys to tie each other up while he knelt by the side of his fallen amigo.

Cut.

Pancho walked away without another word. Take that, you stupid Roumanian, he thought as he dusted off his chaps. But then he heard a cry from one of the starlets. He turned and looked back. Cisco did not move at all. Cisco could not move. Cisco was not conscious.

The unthinkable had happened. Stunned, the cast and crew looked on, helpless. They could not wait for an ambulance so they took the door off one of the sets and put Cisco on it; he came to, and cried out in excruciating pain. They shoved the door in the back of a station wagon and drove an hour and twenty minutes to the nearest hospital, Hollywood Presbyterian. The Cisco Kid had broken his neck. Or the red rock had. In any event, said the doctor after surgery, the Cisco Kid might never walk again.

O Ceesco. O Pancho.

The whole production's shock and sorrow was no doubt genuine. But in truth, the series was over, and everyone was out of work. Cisco was one unpopular *hombre.*

Only Pancho remained loyal. Pancho put their old quarrel aside, and faithfully helped his friend recover. Slowly Cisco's mobility returned, enough to dress himself unaided, enough to walk unaided. But Cisco's days of heroism and señorita-kissing would never come again. The pain alone had furrowed his face. His hair had gone white.

And Pancho? He was a famous Sidekick, but so indelibly identified with Cisco he could never be anyone else's. He had been grinning for so long he had forgotten how to growl and look fierce; this meant he could never again be a Bad Guy. And, even his grinning experience did him no good: he was too old to play roles like Dr. Zodiac Z. Zippe. His career, too, was finished.

O Ceesco. O Pancho.

Their old quarrel was resolved in sorrows and shared losses as their wives and various other women left them, deserted, or divorced and took their assets. Their thankless children had all grown up and gone. The Talking Bull had been right. Out of work, out of luck, aging, insomniac, nursing their old injuries and grudges—Pancho and the Cisco Kid retired to El Rancho Stucco. They became recluses. Even to each other.

Cisco grew grim and silent. He would rise daily, put on his boots with silver spurs, his silver spangled sombrero. He sat at the edge of his narrow bed, perfectly made with hospital corners. He waited for nothing, and nothing happened.

Pancho, against his very nature, grew melancholy. He drank too much in the evenings, but only in the evenings. However, the sun went down earlier and earlier, and El Rancho Stucco seemed bathed in unchanging twilight. His sleep was uneasy, intermittent. In dreams he unwillingly relived the race, thousands cheering, grandstands swaying as boy and beast outraced Death and dust and wind, and time itself, until the goggled albino frog flew by on the white back of Death. How long after that did Pancho and

El Cid ride? Forever? To ride and ride and come only upon the windless void? Pancho woke, fearful, trembling, sweating, shook the *mal sueño* from his mind. Since his defeat by Death, had all else been a dream? *¿Es toda la vida un sueño?* He sat up, feet on the worn floor, his thick-veined hands limp. On these sleepless nights he sought refuge in the library.

In the library the Talking Bull was, metaphorically speaking, everywhere. The horns were over the fireplace. On the desk were two pencil holders and two paperweights made from the hooves of the Talking Bull. The hide had been stretched across two chair frames, and a loveseat. A portrait of the Andalusian El Cid hung on the only wall not covered with bookshelves. On the shelves ten thousand ragged paperbacks sagged against one another, mass market novels from every vacation rental shack that graced every lake or beach or mountain cabin. Many books had lurid covers, buxom women in off-shoulder blouses defying—and succumbing to—steely-eyed men. Many books by Louis L'Amour, Zane Grey, Karl May, and Ned Buntline. Two whole shelves were devoted to editions of Owen Wister's *The Virginian*, and of course O. Henry's *The Cisco Kid*.

Pancho read the books, read all of them eventually, but they gave him scant pleasure, and did not cure his insomnia. If the library could not cure him, perhaps the kitchen might. He padded down the long hall not looking at the framed yellowing pictures of buxom señoritas and smiling studio heads.

He turned on the kitchen light and beheld at the table a single mariachi player. His guitar lay beside him like a corpse. A single cigarette burned in the ash tray, one long gray cinder, lacking even the will to crumble. The guitarist offered no explanation, and perhaps none was needed. The musician's hair was gray with dust; his eyes were sunken, his chin stubbled, and his face gaunt.

Pancho remembered him of course. The Golden Age of Television. Mariachi musicians at the faked fiestas, faux cantinas where the Cisco Kid had smiled at the señoritas, and the comic Sidekick had stayed near the food because he was always so *hongry.*

Pancho put the coffee beans in the grinder and turning away from the guitarist, he attended to his noisy task. He filled the pot at the sink, and dumped the coffee in. When he looked back at the table, dawn eked through the shutters. A dozen Bad Guys had joined the guitarist, including the one who had pushed the fake red rock, breaking Cisco's neck. Some leaned on their forearms, heads on the table. Some sprawled uneasily on rickety kitchen chairs. They all wore black hats.

Pancho did not know how they had come to El Rancho Stucco, but he knew why. They, too, were old, out of work, out of luck, alone, sleepless, nursing their grudges and wounds, wishing their peckers were still strong and firm, and upright, that something was enlarged besides their prostates and their hairy ears. These are old men with much to think about, much to regret. Their aches are as much in the heart as in their arthritic limbs.

To the guitarist Pancho remarked that just as Bad Guys were never singular, so the thought of a lone mariachi was impossible.

The guitarist licked his dry lips. He picked up his guitar and stroked it slowly back to life. He said the rest of them were redeeming their instruments from pawn shops.

So, asked Pancho, firing up the stove, will they be here for breakfast?

* * *

These Bad Guys and mariachis all found solace at El Rancho Stucco. For shelter they built rambling additions and outbuildings, a tin-roofed carport, bunkhouses beamed with lumber, and walled with stucco and concoctions of mud and straw and dung and memory, that old *adobe* of youth, mortared with nostalgia. No one stopped them. Building codes don't apply to El Rancho Stucco. Nothing applies to El Rancho Stucco. It couldn't be inspected or taxed or levied, or insured, or made to comply with laws, saving for gravity and thermodynamics. It was protected by a thick caul of oblivion, the surrounding hills and the chain link fence.

The coming of the Bad Guys and the mariachis gave Pancho not merely company, but purpose. Having relied his entire life on what he'd learned from reckless men of his family, Pancho now turned to what the lovely women had long ago taught him. *La cocina Mexicana.* He re-discovered tastes and techniques. He savored, smiled, sighed and imparted his wisdom to the Bad Guys These tough old hombres learned to cook and Pancho taught them, not all he knows naturally, but some. He replaced their six-guns with *molinillos.*

Their contests are now long delicious duels fought at High Noon. Lunchtime.

"¿You got teeny little *tomatillos* for *cojones.*"

"¡I'll show you! ¡I got real *albondigos!*"

"¿Eh, this loco hombre don't think mine are the best *huevos rancheros?*"

"Sí, and your *cerviche* stinks of dead *pescador.*"

"¡I'll scramble your *rellenos!*"

The contests are deadly serious. The winners will be decided by the look on Pancho's face as he judges their cooking. Bad losers will fling their fry pans out the windows. There is no glass in the windows, no screens either. Only paint-peeling wooden shutters that creak when they are closed at night.

And through these shutters, at midnight, the scent of Pancho's sleeplessness sometimes wafts all over El Rancho Stucco. Seeking consolation from his bad dreams, from the un-summoned memory of Death, the grinning face of the albino frog, Pancho wakes, leaves his bed and pads into the kitchen. The floor tiles are cool on his bare feet. He fires up the old stove. A greasy apron encircles Pancho's girth; wisdom lights up his much-lined face. He soaks the dried peppers in hot water. He grills his chilis. He grinds the spices as he was taught long ago. The scrape of mortar and pestle comforts him. He takes his time. There is no rush. There is no schedule. No timetable, no time at all to speak of. The chilis sear, the spiced, stringy meat in the pot warms. Expertly he flips tortillas, and tastes, tests the molé, to be certain it is correctly seasoned, flavored with the silvery fountains, the laughter of lovely women, the cries of reckless men, spiced with the essence of dried bougainvillea blossoms, infused, in short, with your typical evenings of lost time.

The bewitching fragrance curls, coils, yawns and stretches itself all across El Rancho Stucco. The old horses rouse from their *sueños* of Andalusia. The chickens flutter. The dogs snort, stretch and amble to the house. Even the sheep, dumb as they are, are stirred, but lack of volition keeps them stationary until they hear the goats' bells. Then they follow the goats.

The bells wake wrinkled mariachis from *mal sueños* of marimbas and trumpets and guitars that lie orphaned in pawn shops. Of pawn tickets gone gray, crumbled to dust before their instruments can be redeemed. Everything lost and unredeemed. *¿Es toda la vida* *un sueño?* They are grateful to wake. The musicians throw on their serapes and go to the kitchen.

Aged Bad Guys rouse from bad dreams of holdups gone shamefully awry where they are roughed up by men with no sweat stains, where they are crowded into pasteboard hoosegows. Lonesome, guilty and bereft. *¿Es toda la vida un sueño?* They rub their stubbly chins, slide their feet into huarache sandals, and trudge to the kitchen.

Cisco wakes. He mops his face. He is dreaming of the Red Rock prop that broke his neck. In his dreams he does not live, but neither does he know what it is to die. He rises, makes his narrow bed with hospital corners. He puts the silver sombrero on his white head, pulls on the silver-studded pants, the silver spurred boots. He never forgets he is the Cisco Kid. He strides to the kitchen like the hero he was born to be.

The *frijoles* are on the stove and the *salsa verde* is on the table. The air is seared with cooking chilis, dried grilled peppers of Pancho's ¡olé molé! From the pot of bubbling meat, the fragrance of cumin and coriander tease like the smiles of the first señoritas these old men ever loved. The piquant scent of fresh cilantro is like these girls' remembered breath.

Pleased, Pancho nods to his old amigos, smiles and dishes up delight and consolation. *¿Es toda la vida un sueño?* Perhaps. Perhaps Pancho has not beaten the albino frog on Death, but he has beaten the dream of Death. Though he is unthinkably old, Pancho feels impossibly alive. Senses tingling, he is alert, aware of *toda la vida:* paint as it peels, paperbacks as their spines crack, tumbleweeds as they free themselves from the chain link fence and follow the reckless wind.

Photo Courtesy of Centrum.

Rebecca Brown's twelfth book, *American Romances: Essays*, was released by City Lights in 2009. Other titles include *The Last Time I Saw You, The End of Youth, The Dogs, The Terrible Girls* (all with City Lights), *Excerpts from a Family Medical Dictionary* (Granta and U of Wisconsin), and *The Gifts of the Body* (HarperCollins). A frequent collaborator, she has written numerous texts for dance; a play, *The Toaster*; and *Woman in Ill Fitting Wig*, a book length collaboration with painter Nancy Kiefer. She also co-edited, with Mary Jane Knecht of the Frye Art Musuem, *Looking Together: Writers on Art* (University of Washington Press). Brown's work has been translated into Japanese, German, Italian, Norwegian and Dutch. She lives in Seattle.

Rebecca read her story, *The Evolution of Darkness*, at the inaugural 1999 Bedtime Stories event.

THE EVOLUTION OF DARKNESS

I've always had problems getting to sleep and even once I am asleep, it's rare for me to enjoy a night of calm unbroken rest. When I was little, my grandmother would always come and tuck me in at night. After, she would pull the covers up to my chin and kiss me and say goodnight, she would tell me to close my eyes and go to sleep. I'd close my eyes and feel her cool palm on my forehead and the quiet ease of pressure lifting off the bed as she stood up and turned to leave my room. As soon as she had turned, I'd open my eyes and watch her leave. And as soon as she was at my door, I'd shout my answering, 'Goodnight, Gammy,' and add, 'You can go ahead and stay outside my door again just to make sure I fall asleep.' She would turn, and I would watch the silhouette she threw against the yellow hall light wave goodnight to me. She'd close the door halfway and I would hear her carpet-muffled steps fade down the hall.

Every night this was the same.

She never stood outside my door to hear the even breathing of the starting of my sleep, but I didn't really shout this for her, I shouted it for me, because my voice sounded big in my quiet room, I sounded as if I had courage. I shouted it as a warning that my grandmother was there and that I was strong and unafraid, to say I wouldn't be surprised by the 'it' that filled my room each night when dark encountered by imagination.

I often wanted to ask my grandmother to search through things for me before she left me to face my darkened room alone, to open the closet and shake the coats and sweaters hanging there, lift the blankets and bedcovers and shine a flashlight under my bed, to open my toy trunk and look behind the bookshelves. But I always decided against this because I didn't want her to stir anything up.

Much as I didn't want to find it alone, I didn't want her to find it.

I had my own room on the first floor above the garage. Outside my window I could see trees and shrubs in our yard and the tall wide wall around our house. The wall was huge and thick and it had bits of chipped glass on it to cut robbers when they tried to get in. Sometimes all I could see out of my window was the sharp white glint of moonlight in the pointy jagged glass. But mostly I could see the driveway, wide and smooth, and on nights with a big moon, perfect tiny round stones in it shining. The trees in our yard were fir trees and other kinds, and the fir trees had sharp and fuzzy outlines.

My room poured in with skinny moonlight over my bed. I lay in the faint, cold cool blue light and looked. My closet was across the room from the window and sometimes the closet door was closed at night, and sometimes it was open. When it was open I could see my clothes hanging and they looked grey and black and white and sometimes blue in the dim light. I would look and look at the closet. I could hear the rustling behind the clothes or see the clothes moving. Sometimes I could see it hidden and disguised as clothes. I could see the stiff hard shoulder that was black and white, and legs and the bottoms of feet. I could see it standing in my clothes, tall and quiet, looking at me. I could see tall hats on heads and headdresses going up almost to the ceiling. I wondered when it was going to come out, if it was waiting for me to fall asleep. I wondered if it could see me watching it the way I wished I could see it, because, from where I was, the light shone on it, but went over me. And I wondered if it always waited for people to fall asleep before it came out; and how it knew: if it was just the even breathing, or if it knew some other way too; and sometimes I tried to make my breathing even for a long time to see if I could fake it out and it would start from the closet and I could scream and my grandmother would come and catch it while it was there and get rid of it.

When the closet was closed, I couldn't see it, but I could hear it. I wondered if it could see me through the slanted slats by putting its eyes right up next to them, and I tried to listen to see if I could hear it opening the door on its way out to me.

After my grandmother left me alone, my heart started beating faster. I'd lift my arms out from under the covers and fold my hands together over my neck. That was in case it tried to slash my throat or strangle me, my hands would be there first and I could help myself. And I always kept my eyes closed because somehow I'd come to believe that no one, not even it, ever killed sleeping little girls. Perhaps because sleeping little girls slept through everything and couldn't hear or see or know what had happened and therefore couldn't tell on it. Ignorance was an excuse; it was a sleeping little girl's salvation. I'd lie still and stiff as I could, my legs straight and together, my elbows tucked against my stomach. And I'd try to breathe as quietly as I could, just in case it was being overcautious and wanted to ensure my silence; I'd pretend I was dead. I'd lie and listen to the creaks in the wood, the swishing noise of my head against the pillow, the scrape of branches on the window shutters, the rustle of the crawlies in the rain gutter, the pops and pings of aluminum cooling down around me with the evening. But to me, my eyes clenched closed, my breathing tight and irregular, all these sounds were it.

When I woke up from a dream at night sometimes I'd be screaming and Gammy was there shaking me awake. But sometimes I would wake along, my eyes sprung open, my breath caught; it had touched me and my voice was gone. I was always cold with sweat, and lost. I'd try to figure out where I was. Sometimes I'd remember right off and throw my hands back on my throat and hope, heart racing, that it wouldn't notice I'd woken up. Other times I would cry out loud without thinking, 'Momma! Daddy!' and my grandmother would come and turn on the lights and hold me. I was often afraid after I'd called, regretting that my grandmother was on her way to my room, and I wanted to warn her not to come in, because it might still be there and it would get her too. I always half expected to see the scattering of black gauze wings, the slamming of the closet door, the quick dark shadow yanking back beneath my bed. And though I never did see it, I always knew we'd only missed each other by an instant.

* * *

Many nights I felt I hadn't slept at all, like I'd lain awake the whole night listening to my heart beat, and listening to it. I'd always be surprised to wake in the morning, after having slept a sleep that I'd forgotten. And every morning when I awoke, I did so with relief, having made it through another night. But this relief was only momentary, because it was soon replaced with a weighty sense of self-reprimand. I never woke in the protective pose I'd gone to sleep in. I awoke on my stomach, or curled up with my knees tucked up to my chin. I awoke to sheets and blankets disarrayed; I wondered if this was evidence of a midnight scramble out of which I'd fought my way then, exhausted, fallen back to sleep and forgotten. And though I could never be absolutely sure this wasn't the case, I doubted that it was or else why, I asked myself with a swallow, why had it let me go?

* * *

When I was very young, darkness and my bedtime, like waking and going to the bathroom, were always linked together. I had to go to sleep because 'it was getting dark'. Odd mornings when I woke up early I'd be sent back to bed because 'it wasn't even light yet'. I'd made a horrible mistake by waking when I wasn't supposed to and I'd better get back to bed before something bad happened. I started drawing connections from these facts and I reasoned that my sleepiness was the actual cause of darkness. When I got tired, it got dark. This was my first extended memory and the first memory I have of making a plan.

If I could just stay awake the whole time, it would never be dark and it would be day all the time. I knew I wasn't the only one that didn't like the dark. At night everyone gathered around the fireplace or lamps because that's how you could be warm or read or see who you were talking to. I heard people complain, if too many lights were left on, that you were wasting light. I hated that there wasn't enough to go around and I hated responsibility for it. After all, I was always the one getting sleepy and bringing the dark. No one else ever complained to me and this is one reason I loved them more. I tried to see what it was they did that made them not tired like me. First of all they were bigger and I couldn't be that for a long time. But another thing was, they didn't move as much, they sat still and talked more and read. They also ate more. Then I made my plan to become as much like them as I could so I wouldn't get tired so I wouldn't have to sleep so it would be light. So, for several days, I acted quiet and tried to do what they did. And then when the big day came, I didn't play at all so I would store energy. When I was told to go to bed I was eager and happy because I had a surprise for them. My grandmother tucked me in and I kissed her goodnight. When she left I sat up in my bed just as the room was turning dusky grey. I was happy because any minute they were going to run in and thank me for staying up and keeping the light. I kept looking at the door, expecting to see them coming.

But I was concentrating so hard I didn't notice the change in the light until it was almost too dark to see the door at all. I couldn't believe it was happening. I screamed, 'Momma! Momma! Momma!' I'd stayed awake and everything, but it still got dark. My grandmother came running in. She flipped on the hall light and then the bedroom light and then she was there holding me next to her.

She put my head against her big warm dress and held me. I remember the feel of my tear-wet face against her and I remember the soapy smell of her dress and the wet smell of her body underneath her dress and I remember her smoothing my hair down. I cried, 'I'm sorry, I'm sorry,' over and over again and she said, 'Ssshhh, ssshhhh.' When I settled down she said, 'Honey, you're sweating.' Her voice sounded the same good round way she smelled. She rocked me against her and after a while when I was quiet she loosened her strong arms from me. I pulled away from her a little. 'Now what's this you're so sorry for?' I told her about my plan for making it stay light for everyone and how sorry I was that I couldn't do it and it was dark. Then she pulled me to her again and told me I had nothing to do with it getting dark, it just always got dark and it did before I was born and it would do it after I died. She said it just got dark on everyone and there was nothing stopping it. I told her I didn't like that then, that I was afraid then. And she told me, it's just something you live with and you learn not to think of, of how you're afraid of it, and then maybe you really won't be afraid.

For weeks after that I dreaded the night and I was terrified of going to bed. I couldn't believe there was something no only bigger than me, but bigger than my grandmother and everyone, something that no one liked but there was nothing you could do about. I hated knowing that it was the dark and the whole time I slept, that there was something in the dark I couldn't see. My grandmother kept the hall light on for me after that. I begged her to keep it on the whole night, because what if I woke up and everything was dark, but the light was always out when I woke up in the morning. I hated going to sleep but I hated worse the thought of being awake in the dark, awake and aware of how powerless I was. If I couldn't do anything about it, then I'd rather know as little about it and the thing that lived inside it as I could.

Photo Courtesy of Dan Pelle.

Jess Walter is the author of five novels, including *The Zero*, a finalist for the 2006 National Book Award and *Citizen Vince*, winner of the 2005 Edgar Allan Poe Award for best novel. He has been a finalist for the L.A. Times Book Prize and the PEN USA Literary Prize in both fiction and nonfiction. His books have been *New York Times*, *Washington Post* and NPR best books of the year and are translated into twenty-two languages.

Jess emceed the 2008 Bedtime Stories event themed "Night Hawk," at which he read *A Brief Political Manifesto*. The poem appears in his most current novel *The Financial Lives of the Poets*.

A BRIEF POLITICAL MANIFESTO

I was driving around the packed Costco parking lot
looking for a space and listening to a guy
on NPR talk about the upcoming election
and the irrational voting pattern
of America's growing suburban poor, when I saw one
this woman with four kids—
little stepladders, two-four-six-eight—
waiting to climb in the car while Mom
loaded a cask of peanut butter and
pallets of swimsuits into the back
of this all-wheel drive vehicle
and the kids were so cute I waved
and that's when I saw the most amazing thing
as the woman bent over
to pick up a barrel
of grape juice:
her low-rise pants rose low and right there
in the small of her large back
stretched a single strained string,
a thin strap of fabric, yes,
the Devil's floss, I shit you not
a thong, I swear to God, a thong,
now me, I'm okay with the thong

politically and aesthetically, I'm fine
with it being up there or out there,
or wherever it happens to be.

My only question is:
when did Moms start wearing them?

I remember my mom's underwear.
(Laundry was one of our chores:
we folded those things awkwardly,
like fitted sheets. We snapped them
like tablecloths. *Thwap.*
My sisters stood on one end,
me on the other
and we walked toward each other
twice.

We folded those things
like big American flags,
hats off, respectful
careful not to let them
brush the ground.)

Now I know there are people out there
who constantly fret about
the Fabric of America:
gay couples getting married, violent videos, nasty TV,
that sort of thing.
But it seems to me
the Fabric of America
would be just fine
if there was a little bit more of it
in our mothers' underpants.

And that is the issue I will run on
when I eventually run:
Getting our moms out of thongs
and back into hammocks
with leg holes
the way God
intended.

Mary Guterson is the author of the novels *We Are All Fine Here* (Putnam, 2005), and *Gone to the Dogs* (St. Martin's, 2009). Her work has appeared in numerous publications, including literary journals, magazines, blogs, and anthologies. For several years, she was a regular commentator for Seattle's NPR affiliate (KUOW-FM 94.9), and appeared as a recurring guest on that station's weekly satirical news show "Rewind." She currently lives in Los Angeles, where she speaks at conferences and workshops.

Mary read her story, *Field Trip*, at the 2006 event themed "Night Watch."

FIELD TRIP

The last thing I wanted to do was chaperone Kyle's fourth grade field trip, but I said yes anyway because, for one, I needed the good mommy points, and for two, my gut told me I should go.

My gut is never wrong.

For instance, my gut told me not to marry Marcus, and look what happened there. Twelve years of marriage and he leaves me for fat Sheila. God, all those years counting calories and as it turns out, Marcus goes for the fat girls.

But the field trip.

Well, first thing, buttoned-up Mr. Harrison asks if I'd mind sitting next to the little retarded girl on the bus, the one none of the other kids'll go near. Except he doesn't say "retarded," he says, "our little Hayley, here." And then he points to this girl with crooked teeth and a round doughy face who is at that very moment picking her nose. What was I going to say?

It was a very long ride.

Kyle totally ignored me.

Hayley dug for China up her nostrils and sniffed at her armpits.

Mr. Harrison kept shouting, "Feet out of the aisle!"

I watched the black grime at the base of the window and counted cars.

After a while, we hit the south side of town and then there was nothing to see but old warehouses, train tracks and telephone wires, and above it all, the gray sky sagging, threatening to fall. We pulled into the middle of nowhere and the bus stopped.

"Ever been to the Flight Museum before?" I asked Hayley.

The girl lifted one black shoe off the ground and sniffed at the bottom of it.

"Stop that," I said.

Basically, I'd lost patience with everyone, retarded or not.

The kids trampled off the bus and into the parking lot where Mr. Harrison was dividing them into small groups. No one seemed to be missing me. Then a voice called out.

"You coming?"

It was the bus driver, his eyes fixed on me through the rear view mirror.

"Yeah," I said.

"Now there's some enthusiasm."

I made my way up the bus aisle.

"My husband's romping around South America with another woman," I said to him. "And I'm here."

The bus driver had silver hair shorn close to his big head and a pot belly Marcus wouldn't have approved of.

"Maybe he'll get kidnapped by a drug cartel," he said.

"Right," I said.

"Hey, anything's possible."

I stepped off the bus. Mr. Harrison was poking at his clipboard with a pen.

"Ah, Mrs. Denver," he said to me. "If you could take this group."

He nodded his head toward conspicuous Hayley in her red sweat pants and black shoes, standing amid an indistinguishable blur of boys.

"Remember what I told you," Mr. Harrison was saying to the boys. "And Hayley, you stick with Mrs. Denver."

The blur of boys took off toward the museum doors.

"Stick with me, Hayley," I said.

At that, she ran to join the others.

* * *

In all our married life, we'd had only one fight. It was about a tree in our back yard, a tree I thought would one day fall on the house and kill us both. Marcus, on the other hand, found it disturbing that I found one huge fir tree in the center of our suburban lawn so disturbing. He said, that's why people live here.

We finally decided to hire an arborist.

The tree man showed up on a Wednesday, wearing a plaid shirt and jeans and glasses. He looked at the tree and tapped at it and studied the surrounding trees and took some measurements with a tape measure.

"Hard to say," he said, finally.

That night, we had the fight. Marcus followed me around the house, saying that I was going off the deep end now, worrying about everything under the sun, what next? Was a meteor going to fall on the house? Did I want him to build us a bomb shelter?

The day after Marcus left me for Sheila, I called the arborist.

"How much to take it down?" I asked.

The tree man came back the following week. This time he wore grimy gray jeans hacked off just below the knees, a pair of iron-toed boots, and a navy watch cap. In place of the glasses, a pair of safety goggles. He climbed the tree with a rope, kicking at the bark with a pair of cleats, then chain-sawed the whole thing down, piece by piece, hanging from the tree's core like a superhero.

In retrospect, I think Marcus and I needed a few more fights. I should have listened to my gut on that one, too, because, in truth, there were quite a few things that used to piss me off.

* * *

I had no interest in the movie on space flight Mr. Harrison was herding everybody into the theater to watch, so I walked around the museum instead, taking in the sights. Of course, there wasn't anything to see except things having to do with space and flight. Marcus would have loved it, all of the old engines, and photographs, and displays of uniforms and dehydrated food products. Marcus was probably eating a dehydrated food product at that very moment in the wilds of South America, fat Sheila barefoot by his side.

I decided to look for the gift shop and see what they had to purchase on Marcus' credit card. I made my way through the freezing museum, through the cavernous fake hangar where a bunch of old airplanes sat permanently grounded, past the tin can looking thing someone had once taken into space. I asked a security guard in a burgundy jacket for directions to the gift shop.

"Just past the simulator," he said, pointing. "Then take a left."

The simulator turned out to be a tiny, dark room fixed up to look like the inside of a space ship. In the front of the room, three plastic orange chairs faced a dashboard covered with levers and gauges. On the wall, a huge fake picture window looked out on a fake, star-lit sky moving past, so that, if you had an imagination, you could imagine you were flying right through it. I sat in one of the chairs and watched the fake stars fly by, one endless loop of night, and as I watched, I thought about the fact that I was spending all my nights alone in a big empty bed while Marcus was sleeping with Sheila. I didn't want to be alone the rest of my life. I wondered if anyone would ever love me again. Right about then, that simulation room seemed to be just about the most depressing place in the universe. I needed some daylight.

I made it back to the movie theater just as the kids came streaming out, screaming and socking at one another. Hayley was the last to emerge. She ran her fingers along the wall and whispered God knows what to herself.

"Did you like the movie?" I asked her.

"No," she said.

Mr. Harrison clapped his hands three times.

"Everyone!" he said. "We'll be touring the airplanes in the hangar area next. Remember, hands to yourselves at all times."

The kids shoved each other down the hallway while Hayley let them pass. Then she turned and pressed her face against the wall.

"Come on, Hayley," I said. "Here we go."

She glanced in my direction, turned her face back to the wall and banged her forehead against it.

"Hayley," I said. "You're going to hurt yourself."

She banged her forehead again, harder this time.

"Hayley!" I said. "Please! Quit doing that!"

I set a hand on the girl's shoulder. Hayley turned, gave me a look of exasperation, and whacked me in the bicep. Then she returned to her forehead banging. Where was Mr. Harrison? Where was the security guard? Where on earth was Hayley's mother? I should have stayed home. My gut had let me down.

"She's not mine," I said to a man walking toward us.

I realized he was the bus driver.

"Maybe I should get the teacher?" he asked.

From his tone of voice, you'd think he watched children whack their foreheads against walls every day.

"Oh, God, yes," I said. "Thank you."

He headed off and Hayley slowed her banging and a minute later when the bus driver returned with Mr. Harrison, she was only standing there, doing nothing. The teacher leaned in to talk in a soft voice to Hayley.

"I don't want to go with her," Hayley was saying.

Mr. Harrison whispered some more.

"I won't," Hayley said. "I won't go with that lady there."

Mr. Harrison took Hayley by the arm.

"I'm sorry, Mrs. Denver," he said. He didn't sound sorry at all. He sounded slightly disgusted by my lack of parenting skills. He sauntered away with Hayley hanging easily in his grip. Without at all wanting to, it seemed I was about to cry.

"Would you like to go outside?" the bus driver asked me.

"Okay," I said.

I followed him out the door of the museum. We looked around for someplace to sit but there wasn't a bench anywhere in sight, so we sat on the ground, leaning against the museum wall. There was nothing to look at except an empty stretch of road, a couple of old pink buildings across the way, and the big yellow bus, stranded and waiting in the center of the asphalt. By then, I'd caught my breath.

"Remind me never to do this again," I said.

He lit a cigarette and handed it to me. I'd never been a smoker.

"No, thanks," I said.

I stared at nothing.

"I'm not too good at conversation," I told him.

"Thanks for the warning."

He took a drag of the cigarette and blew out the smoke.

"You have a kid," he said. "That's a conversation piece."

"He hates me."

"Not big with children, are you?" he said.

A car pulled up to the front of the museum, stopped to let a woman out, then drove off again. The woman went inside the museum. And then I couldn't help myself. I started to cry. I wiped at my face with the back of my hand. The bus driver dug around in his shirt pocket and came up with a tissue.

"I am one boring person," I said.

"No kidding. I'm falling asleep over here."

"God, how did I get here?" I asked.

The bus driver looked at me.

"I drove you?" he said.

A couple of crows hopped along the asphalt a dozen feet away, then took off into the air again.

"Hey, we can't all go to South America," the bus driver said.

I looked at the bus driver. He looked at his watch.

"Two more hours," he said.

I thought of all the things I'd never done in my life. Never been to South America. Never slept with anyone but Marcus. Never smoked a cigarette. I looked at the bus.

"You like driving that thing?" I asked.

The bus driver looked at me. He had nice eyes. I didn't at all mind his potbelly.

"Come on," he said.

We walked to the bus. The bus driver opened the door and gave me the driver's seat. He turned the key and the engine rumbled into action, loud and eager, and nearly, but not quite, drowning out the sound of my reliable gut.

"Give it some gas," the bus driver told me then. "Drive."

Photo Copyright © Dave Fisher.

Karen Fisher's debut novel, *A Sudden Country*, earned numerous awards, including the Sherwood Anderson Foundation Award and the VCU First Fiction award, and was a finalist for many others, including the L.A. Times Art Seidenbaum and PEN/Faulkner Awards for fiction. She lives with her family on an island off the coast of Washington.

Karen read her story, *Mud Night*, at the 2006 event themed "Night Watch."

MUD NIGHT

The kids were sick of the back seat.

My husband Dave had moved us all to Washington State a few years before, only to become a poster child for Seasonal Affective Disorder. A week before spring break, *he* had broken. We had to leave. Somewhere. Anywhere with sun.

Ellen wanted Paris. She was eleven, a born artist who saw everything as reds and blues and pinks, the painted fingernails of waitresses, the shapes of signs and eyeglasses. She always knew what to wear, and how best to appear normal, even in a family that could not seem to buy Kleenex, or grow a lawn, or get the right smelling detergent.

Grant wanted Hawaii. He was golden, nine years old, and lived for pure velocity, concrete, ramps, and pipes. He was a skater with a dream to surf. In our world of dark forest and gravel, he dreamed of smooth curves, waves, anything bright and fast. Lachlan, who was seven, loved sitting inside with anything small and electronic.

But we were liberally educated, self-employed, downwardly mobile, and somehow always unable to deliver those things our children most desired. Transcendence for us was always somewhere outside, the more remote and difficult to achieve, the better. My mother, having heard the phrase "alternative lifestyle," used it now when explaining us to friends. All were entertained by her stories of us. We lived such interesting lives. On a farm, on a boat, in a tiny island cabin without power. Milling our own logs to lumber. What would we think of next?

Dave said, "Let's drive down to the desert."

"No, Dad," Ellen had said.

"It'll be fun. We'll see wild horses. We'll lie in the sun."

We'd packed our truck with camping gear.

Before children I was always glad to go somewhere to camp with Dave, but now my happiness relied on rare moments when all of us were satisfied. I said, "We'll buy a GameBoy."

The sun came out the day we left. Sky darkened, going south. We drove down through snow and drizzle, hit California in monsoon-like rain. In Indio, drove through dust storms, night lightning. Made camp and watched the clouds roll in. It rained. Black water roared down muddy washes. We read aloud under dripping tarps. We made Indian gambling games from sticks. Woke to frost at Joshua Tree, raced record downpours in Death Valley. In an effort to cheer us all up, I'd at last insisted on getting a hotel in Lone Pine. We'd get a good night's sleep, I said, and get warm in the hot tub. But renovators had left an air compressor in the room underneath us. It roared on and off all night, and the hot tub was ringed in lines of greasy black like a textbook cross-section of the epochs of the earth. It proved Dave's insistence. The best things in life could not be bought, they were all outside somewhere. The very best required four-wheel drive.

But whatever it was—never mind natural beauty, just a little sun, or even *warmth*—we hadn't come close to finding it on this trip, and Dave had been dragging out the miles returning home on narrow mountain roads, still in hope of something that would satisfy. He'd bought a copy of *Hot Springs of the West* that morning when we'd stopped for coffee. Now I was driving, and the audio recording of *Lemony Snickett* had ended, Grant and Lachlan were squabbling to the theme from *Lord of the Rings*, cut with electronic sword-like noises. Grant grabbed for the GameBoy. Lachlan yelled. Ellen thumped Grant and Grant yelled and Ellen yelled and then we both yelled from the front seat for everyone to be quiet.

"Just get along for one more day," I said, "We're on our way home." I was headed for I-5, ready to lay down miles, get a hotel, end up home in time to do the laundry and go shopping for those little snacks that made me feel so good since I had abandoned my objections to individually packaged items, and started putting them in the kids' school lunches.

"Listen to this one," Dave said. "Hunt Hot Springs, near the town of Big Bend. Delightful rock pools on Pitt River near Mount Shasta. Elevation 2,000 feet."

I glanced at the page he showed me, then at him.

I could say no. I should say no. But then vacation would be over, along with Dave's dreams of warmth and wilderness redemption, and it would be my fault.

"O.K.," I said. "But *then* we go straight home."

* * *

By nightfall, we'd taken three highways, each smaller and darker and windier than the last. Big Bend was a dead-end town, at the end of a long spur winding down toward the river. Dave was driving. "Read those instructions again," he said.

I read what he'd read to me that morning. Then silently read further. *The dirt road has deteriorated badly making it very rough even for 4WD. Consider hiking in.* I said, "Did you see that warning at the bottom?"

He said, "That's just for low-clearance vehicles."

We had descended, by then, from tall forest through clear-cuts and into scrubby steep-walled valley. Our headlights slid across forlorn trailers, rotting plywood cabins. Barking dogs chained to abandoned cars, the boom-and-bust wasteland with all its human refuse. No natural beauty here. I thought of Lachlan's Game Boy, of evil Sauron's charred and smoking forests. We'd lived in logging country once before, knew the world was not black and white, knew both sides of all good arguments. But I also knew we'd look like owl-loving liberals slipping through enemy lines. This was some tough country.

The guidebook said a single store. We saw it, crossed the bridge. I read by flashlight. "...first fork to the left—"

Dave braked hard, backed up. We rocked in our seats.

"Slow down, *Daaad*," Ellen said, as I read, but he was cranking left as directed, and I *did* see the muddy trough, and the muddy road that followed, but Dave gunned it, careening down hub-deep through pin oak and manzanita, headlights flaring through a herd of cattle. They parted, cows and calves leaping up and into scrubland on both sides as we roared, fishtailed, spinning, spinning, slower and slower down a road as narrow as a flume, nowhere to turn and losing momentum. Trees gave way to a clearing, a sea of pocked and tilted mud. In slow motion we swam through, slower, slower. Mud thundered against wheel wells, rained onto the windshield with even the Game Boy ominously silent. And then we were through, and onto a patch of higher ground.

We got out of the truck, stared into the dark.

Back under the dome light, we looked at the book, and looked into the dark again.

"I think that was the junction," Dave said. "I think we passed it."

"I don't care what we passed," I said. "We're not going down there."

"Let's just look."

We skirted through a patch of oak. A little moon stood above the mist, and by its light we could easily see the right hand road got worse. Also, that a small black truck was stuck there and abandoned. We tried the left hand road. Moonlight shone on puddles as big as ponds, on the melted tracks of skidders. Not even cows had come down here.

Dave said, "Let's turn around."

We got in. Dave started the engine, gunned it backwards at a wild slant, then launched forward, down in a hard right turn through the sea of mud. The truck slewed, slowed, stalled, wheels still spinning. He switched the engine off.

He said, "We're screwed."

"Great," Ellen said. "Why did we even *take* this road?"

I opened the door. The dome light shone on stinking gumbo, deep gray clay and manure. I stepped out. My shoes slipped into deep pocked holes. Fetid geysers squirted up my pant legs and then the yielding clay formed around my feet with an amazing suction. *Splock.* I pulled free, took another step. *Splock. Splock.*

Out the window, Ellen called, "Oh, mom, your shoes!"

Dave said, "I can't believe I did this. Why didn't you stop me from doing this?"

* * *

Into the silence that eventually followed, Lachlan said, "Where will we sleep?"

Dave said, "If it rains tonight, we're really *really* screwed."

We opened the tailgate. The dog jumped out. We tossed chunks of firewood into the slurry for stepping stones, carried the kids to land.

"There's a ring around the moon," Dave said. "It's going to rain."

We got out the tarp. We put the kids in a fireman's line, passed out duffels, tents, foam pads, cold box, guitar, sleeping bags, until we found the mattock and the crate of tools. Dave set to work, in hope of something.

I found a clearing in the woods, got out our tent. The kids, by then, were rising to this occasion.

"No, Grant, you carry this one. Lachlan you carry this," Ellen said. "Mom, do we need all the duffels?"

"No. Let's tarp them. Look at the trees with the moon."

Ellen said, "It's actually really pretty here."

"Is this about as stuck as we've ever been?" Grant asked.

"Yes, *duh*," Ellen said.

I said, "Not many dads are able to get people quite this stuck."

"What time is it?"

"About midnight."

"More like mud-night," Grant said.

We laughed.

"You guys are great," I said. "I'm sorry we were yelling."

"It's O.K.," Ellen said. "Anyway, I wouldn't like it if you guys were just cheesy. I definitely wouldn't like a cheesy mom."

"What's a cheesy mom?"

"All fake and boring."

Lachlan asked, "Will it rain tonight?"

I said, "It might."

"If it rains, what will happen to the truck?"

"It'll get more stuck," I said. "We might not get out for a long time."

"*How* long?" Ellen asked.

"If it really rains, it could be many days."

"Cool," said Grant.

Clearly being stuck in the mud was not worse than being stuck in school.

"Then the truck will sink?" Lachlan asked.

"Yes it will," I said, snapping the poles together, squinting in the moonlight to see which were black and which were gold.

Stricken, he said, "But the *Game Boy* is inside."

I saw his vision, pouring rain and the mud slowly rising, sealing doors, covering windows, oozing over the roof in cartoon bubbles. I laughed. "Not that deep," I said. "The Game Boy's safe."

Dave came back through the trees. The tent was up. Our things lay tarped against the coming rain.

"Well?"

"Even if I could jack it up and get under it, I'd only gain a couple of feet." How long would it take to cross a sea of mud two feet at a time? He said, "We might as well enjoy those hot springs."

* * *

We found flashlights, towels, and followed the dog down the slippery road. Forty yards away the small black truck, now companion to our own, was also a warning: smashed glass, garbage, moldy seats. The road got steeper. Grant's flashlight beam swept over a desolate tan sedan with four flat tires, seats gone, trunk sprung.

Our big red truck was the first good thing that Dave and I had earned together—it was work and play, firewood, construction, hauling hay; it was dump runs, ski trips, camping. It was literally a part of us. Now each bend toward the river brought another metal corpse, someone's joyride, some dad's borrowed car, some nice young couple up from U.C. Davis for whom that day had ended with someone yelling, "Why didn't you stop me?" All those cars. All those fatal desires.

"In any reasonable place, there'd have been a sign," I said. Even with the moon and oaks I'd sensed the sinister possibility that the people of Big Bend had divined our various weaknesses, were waiting, wondering what the night had trapped.

We found the pools, described accurately, very pleasant. I sat imagining the coming day and who we'd find and how they'd read our muddy clothes, our straight white teeth, our uncut hair. Dave's boots had fallen out the back of the truck when we'd lost the tailgate in Death Valley, and all he had were Tevas. We had forty dollars, and the Visa wouldn't save us.

* * *

In our tent, we lay awake.

Dave kept sighing. The dog growled, then quieted. Rain came and passed. The children breathed. I'd almost gone to sleep when Dave said, "I can trade the gun."

"What *gun?*"

He'd brought his pistol, he explained. That cheap Saturday Night Special he'd bought that first year we'd sold Christmas trees. He'd thrown it in at the last minute.

* * *

In the morning, we left the dog and kids with bacon, walked the road a mile to find the store. A man who looked like Willie Nelson was opening it. He said his name was Freddy. Freaky Freddy.

"Hot springs," he said. We were both head-to-toe in mud.

We admitted it.

"Four-wheel drive?"

We admitted that, too.

"That's your first mistake." He said, "Bill's got a skidder, but he won't go down there now."

We talked. Shrugged, sighed. Identical men, each three hundred pounds and missing teeth, shuffled forward to buy a case of Pepsi. We nodded, watched, talked a little more. With inspired staging, I told Dave I should get back to the kids, they'd be wondering where we were.

"You got *kids* up there?"

"Yeah," I smiled and shrugged. "They're O.K., though. They're pretty tough campers. I think we'll be all right till spring."

Dave said, "You know, I do have a gun I could trade someone for help getting out."

"Well," Freddy said, "let's see who else we know."

* * *

Gaylord and Jim were both on disability and showed up from across the road to see the gun. By midday we had ropes and strapping, logs and chains and strips of cyclone fencing, trucks and ATVs. We were all good friends and I'd decided I probably wouldn't be all that unhappy if we just ended up in Big Bend.

Almost too soon we were out. Gaylord invited us to look at all his guns. By the time we'd finished borrowing his hose, the only deep thing left was gratitude.

Back on the highway we pulled off at Shasta rest area, the Dodge still shedding lumps of clay, our clothes and shoes now stiff and ludicrously heavy. We opened the camper and looked in: tools, tent, duffel. It was hard to tell what color any of it might have been. The muddy dog jumped down. We got out a muddy picnic for our muddy kids, clomped over to a spigot by the sidewalk. Clean water poured into a tidy metal drain. We scrubbed, watching clean people get out of clean cars to walk their clean leashed dogs, escort clean children to the restroom. They all looked carefully away, so as not to encourage us. Maybe this was the real divide— nothing to do with politics or money or education, with what you cut down in your life or left standing, but everything to do with who stayed on the wide roads, and who ventured off them.

I grinned and called the dog.

"Those were good hot springs," Dave said. "We should go again sometime."

Grant agreed. He said, "It was kind of fun getting stuck."

"I can't believe his name was actually Gaylord," Ellen said, who had been almost fatally teased that year by a girl who liked, inexplicably, to call her by that name. And now Gaylord was our hero. He'd said maybe after all that rain, they ought to put up a sign.

But what sign would have convinced us, when no amount of money buys transcendence, and you can't get there without four-wheel drive?

Photo Copyright © Jason Teeples.

Deb Caletti is a National Book Award Finalist whose books are published and translated worldwide. In addition to other distinguished recognition, Deb has also been a PEN USA Literary Award finalist, and has received the Washington State Book Award. Her novels include *The Queen of Everything; Honey, Baby, Sweetheart; The Nature of Jade;* and *The Secret Life of Prince Charming,* among others. Her seventh book with Simon & Schuster, *Stay,* will be released in 2011. Paul G. Allen's Vulcan Productions (*Hard Candy, Far From Heaven*) and Foundation Features (*Capote, Stone of Destiny*) have also partnered to develop Deb's novels into a film series titled *Nine Mile Falls.* She lives with her family in Seattle.

Deb read her story, *Zebra Gloves and Sun Protection Factor 15,* at the 2005 event themed "Moonstruck."

ZEBRA GLOVES AND SUN PROTECTION FACTOR 15

Anna is balancing too many things, as usual. A grocery bag on one hip, purse on her shoulder, keys in her hand.

"Can I help?" Will says, as he always does, after she's put everything down.

"It's fine," she says.

"Tough day?"

"The usual." Anna knows she's using the favorite weapon of the passive aggressive—the two-word response. They'd fought the night before, the usual argument about how Will never listens. Anna has not been looking forward to coming home. Driving here tonight, she had that feeling she gets sometimes, where she imagines herself checking in to the Ramada Inn she passes, or taking an apartment in a place they'd never find her or even think to look. Anna sighs.

"Janey's babysitting. At the Sarasohn's," Will says. See? He will doesn't even say a word about her sigh. But *that's* the favorite weapon of the partner of the passive aggressive—not noticing.

"Is it bad if I say I'm glad?" Anna asks. She rolls her neck, rubs it with her hand.

Janey is their long legged seventeen-year-old, whose emotional volume is always lately set on high. That morning she accused Anna of being overprotective, then yelled at Roscoe when he escaped outside after she'd left the back door open

"Glad that she's gone? Not bad, just human," Will says. He turns off the television, tosses the remote control onto the couch, and helps Anna unload the groceries, which tells her both that he is guilty and that he loves her. He folds up the bag - flap down, then in half, tucks it under the sink in his ordered way as Anna tries not to shrivel in the annoyance one can feel in the presence of an engineer.

"Did you see?" he says.

"See what?" His voice is hopeful, happy, but what comes to her mind first is some image of the car with a new dent, some crisis.

"The moon. Full moon. Lunar madness." He wiggles his eyebrows up and down. "Zebra gloves."

She understands just what this means and smiles in spite of herself. Will sees the smile, and takes her hand. He leads her through the living room, past their bookshelf and Janey's tennis shoes in the hall. Roscoe, who only a moment ago was snoring and doing his dog-dream flinching, rises suddenly to follow as if the sleeping thing had all been a ruse to disguise his ever-present alertness. They step out into the night, onto the porch, and Will shuts the door so as not to let the cold air in—he's careful like that. Whoever said that the things you fall in love with are the ones that'll drive you craziest later knew what he was talking about, but Anna doesn't want to think about that anymore. Because she sees that Will is right. The moon is full, alabaster white, and already it's like Anna sets something down. All the things she's been balancing just rest in their places in mid-air. She sighs again, but this time it's different. A letting go sigh, not a holding on one. She leans against the railing, remembers that Ramada Inns don't have bathrobes, and that's what she likes best in a hotel.

Will rings his arms around her from behind and they stand together, the three of them, Roscoe keeping watch for Ned Chaplin's cats. The night is rich with the smell of burning leaves, even though there are no burning leaves. It's the smell of singed Halloween pumpkin lids, slightly smoky, the smell of change, October cold. Next door, Olivia Watson's bedroom light is on. Olivia Watson has lived alone so long that the presence of other people annoys her. She is always complaining about something - their garbage cans or Ned Chaplin's cats peeing in her yard. Across the street Anna can see the Sarasohn's house, where Janey is babysitting. It's good that Mark and Gina have gone out, Anna thinks. The other day, Anna saw Gina Sarasohn sobbing on her front step. *I can't take it anymore*, she'd told Anna. *He outnumbers me, all by himself.* You could hear Sam, their toddler, screaming behind the door, the thuds of pounding heels. Anna remembers those days.

Will's hands move up under her sweater. "There aren't even any stripes yet," she says.

"We could always do it twice," he suggests, and Anna swats his arm.

"Food first," she says.

"I've got to go feed Ned's cats."

"I still can't picture the guy in Hawaii," Anna says.

"Maybe he'll stay alone in his room watching re-runs of the MacNeil Lehrer report."

"Maybe he'll get laid," Anna says.

"Fat chance," Will says. They both laugh. It's funnier than it seems. Ned is the size and shape of the old Kingdome.

The house fills with the smell of butter and garlic. Anna pours some wine. They eat dinner with more delicacy than usual. Their fight is gone, and there is relief between them. It's if they'd had a guest stay with them they both hated and who's finally left.

"Come on," Will whispers.

Roscoe rises to follow them.

"Stay," Will says, and Roscoe sighs through his nose, lays down, a disappointed chin on his paws.

When Anna opens the bedroom door and Will turns the blinds so that the moonlight lays Venetian stripes across the bed, it all begins to slip from her - the burnt-out fridge light bulb, the clunk sound her car made that morning when she shifted gears. Her boss's yellowed, nicotine fingernails, her mother's age spots, Roscoe's weeping tear ducts—they're all disappearing. It's just this darkness, save for the moonlight. He slips her blouse off her shoulders and her skin is pale in the light. Out of coffee, car insurance due, furnace filters, and five servings of vegetables a day, all going. IRA's, the CPA, ISP's, whatever those are, gone.

There's the schwick of a matchstick struck against sandpaper, the smell of melting wax trying hard to be something citrus. The buttons of his shirt, familiar skin. He lays her down into the moonlight, into the stripes. Lifted now, raised into luminous beams and carried off are her daughter's criticisms, the could have done betters, why did I, why didn't I, the layers of shame a life builds like velvet dust behind furniture, thick enough to run your finger through. And farther back, deeper still, those things go, too—Anna as a child, a hairbrush smacked on the back of her hand, a day at the beach, the smell of Sea 'N Ski lotion, sand in the potato chips.

All vanished, into drowsy moonlit magic. She wears a striped suit on her body. The lines curve this way as she turns, that way. They hug her like a cat suit. He moves over her, and he too is striped, transformed and alien, a mask over part of his face. He runs his hand over her zebra striped boots. She holds a zebra glove in the air and turns her arm for them to admire.

The moonlight creeps under the closed doors of her street, slips into dark corners, shoves aside the flimsy, imposter glow of streetlights. It spreads its white potion, liquid lunacy. The light draws Olivia Watson to her back patio, barefooted and in the chenille robe her children gave her last Christmas. She looks up into the sky, wonders if there is healing power in ancient things. Enough, maybe, to stop the cancer in her. She drops her robe to the pebbled cement littered with pine needles, lets the light bathe her, imagines it soaking deep inside. Her children would die if they saw what she was doing, but there are many things they don't know about her and her old body. She stands there naked and alone, her chin tilted upward. She makes promises, at the same time that Mark and Gina Sarasohn park the car on a quiet street, the moon shining large and round in their windshield as they fumble and undress and contort themselves with hot-cold galactic passion and conceive a second child. Gina's back against the chilled, dewy window is not enough to stop the feeling that wells within her right then, the mysterious need, the pull, some insanity amidst the sanity, or maybe the other way around. Right then as she cries out, one of Ned Chaplin's cats cries out, too, somewhere around the block, that half-scream terror/ecstasy of mating, and Roscoe's ear twitches with weary knowing. And right then, too, Janey tucks Sam into bed. She turns off his lamp, which is shaped like a cowboy boot. Golden light falls onto his blonde head and he is so beautiful that Janey feels her throat close. She's actually crying, she can't believe it, but she is, and for a moment she understands what it means to love a child.

Only the essence of Anna is there. The very last holdouts have left—dressing room mirror visions and *lose five pounds*, and *If I lay this way he won't see*. It's just succulence and vividness and now.

He folds into her and their black and white ribbons meld. New forms, curves, art. Out the window in the sky is the red light from an airplane. Flight 306, Seattle to Honolulu. The woman next to Ned Chaplin shifts in her seat, turns a page of her magazine. The cabin lights are off, and suddenly she gives up, slides the magazine closed, turns off the column of yellow shining on her page. She sighs, turns her head to look out the window. Ned puts the plastic safety card back in the seat pocket in front of him.

"You could almost touch it," he says of the moon.

The woman smiles. She leans close to him in the darkness. "You smell really good," she says.

It's Ned's Hawaiian Tropic Sun Protection Factor 15, which he's applied early on a whim. His heart starts beating fast. As soon as they are free to move about the cabin, Ned will reach into his bag in the overhead bin and retrieve the little box of Tic Tacs he knows he has there somewhere.

Anna's heart, too, is beating fast. "Oh God," she cries. She holds on tight with her zebra gloves, wraps her zebra striped legs tight against his zebra striped back.

Anna awakens in the night. The moon has moved to the other side of the room. Now it is just the dresser that looks different, the door that leads to the bathroom. But that's all right. A transformation may be lasting or fleeting, Anna understands. But what's important is to know it's possible.

Photo Courtesy of Charles Robb.

Candace Robb is the author of two mystery series featuring medieval sleuths, the *Margaret Kerr Mysteries* and the *Owen Archer Mysteries*. Candace came to the Northwest straight from graduate school in medieval literature to work as a technical writer. In the wee hours before work she used her background in the times of Chaucer to create a one-eyed archer and an apothecary's wife in *The Apothecary Rose*, book one in the Owen Archer mysteries. In July 2010 Crown published her first historical novel (non-crime), *The King's Mistress*, under the pen name Emma Campion.

Candace was born in the Blue Ridge Mountains of North Carolina, grew up in Cincinnati, and has lived most of her adult life in Seattle, which she and her husband love for its combination of natural beauty and culture. She enjoys walking, hiking, and gardening, and practices yoga and vipassana meditation. She travels frequently to Great Britain.

Candace read her story, *The Cat Burglar*, at the 2003 event themed "In the Wee Hours."

THE CAT BURGLAR

Close your eyes and imagine you're in bed, cocooned in a warm, fluffy comforter. Say you'd worked out in the garden all day and taken a long, hot bath before turning in. Your muscles are relaxed and warm, your mind fuzzy with sleep. It's one of those wonderful moments when you wake on turning over and check the clock to discover you have hours yet to sleep. You snuggle down even deeper. Delicious.

Creeeeeeeeeeak. Creeeeeeeeeeeeeeeeeak. The floorboards in the bedroom doorway. Is Charlie up? I snake my hand along the soft mattress, find my husband's thigh, and my heart pounds, drowning out all sound even as I hold my breath. A burglar? Did I forget to turn on the alarm system? There's another sound now, but I can't quite make it out. If I don't move… But it's obvious that the two long, parallel mounds beneath the comforter are a sleeping couple. I inch the covers down until my eyes are exposed. Soft light spills down the hallway from the bright porch light, illuminating the walls, paintings, furniture—no intruder standing over us. Now I recognize our cat Agrippa's heavy tread and asthmatic breathing. He's oof-oofing as he settles beneath the bed.

That's not comforting. He hides from *people*.

I jab my toes into my slippers, wrap my bathrobe around me, and head out of the room.

A ghostly white face appears in the kitchen doorway, resolving into our ginger cat Puck. He wants me to come to the kitchen, but first I check the burglar alarm panel—it's armed—at least whatever is spooking the cats isn't human.

In the kitchen Puck shows me that all three sets of kitty bowls are empty. A hungry night. But he's not begging for food, he's now leading me away. I remember the mouse who used to leave a trail of their food that disappeared beneath the fridge. Oh no, not again. But I see no trail, just bowls licked clean.

We both look over our shoulders as we hear the cat flap snap shut down in the media room, and then we take off to confront the intruder. I flip on the spotlights and blind—our youngest kitty, Ariel, returning from her nightly prowl. Puck smells her and hisses. She coos at him. He whacks her, and she pats his rump as she sprints past. Nothing unusual in their greeting.

While Ariel heads up to discover the empty bowls, Puck and I search the downstairs. I get a flashlight to check the laundry room where the three musketeers often corner their prey in the tight spot behind the water heater, but I find nothing. Chilly and shaken by my imagination, I climb the stairs, turning off lights as I go, and slip back into bed. Ariel leaps onto the bed, curls up on Charlie, and is asleep in an instant. I don't fall asleep again till after Puck wakes Charlie for breakfast.

In the following days two things puzzle us: Agrippa takes up residence beneath the guestroom bed except for timid forays to the food bowl and outside to do his business. And every morning the food bowls are licked clean.

Then, on the third day, as I climb the stairs from my office, I spy Sylvester, the feline bully of the neighborhood, sauntering out of my kitchen!

A brief digression. This is a large, fluffy black and white cat who is scruffy but well fed. When he first began to come round I thought he was cute and harmless, and gave him the name Sylvester because he looks like an overweight version of the cat who tormented Tweety Bird. He turned out to be the neighborhood bully. I despise him even more for having fooled me at the beginning.

Sylvester freezes when he sees me—he KNOWS I'm not fond of him—and then dashes into the living room, sliding as he tries to brake and turn on the hardwood floors but his furry paws fail him and he thuds into the glass coffee table. He's up, shaking his head and skitters down the hallway. Ariel, who'd been sleeping beneath the table, just blinks and looks confused as I take off after the shaggy intruder. He's leapt up onto our bed! How well he knows the layout of the house.

"How dare you!" I shout.

He leaps down on the far side and dashes beneath and out, down the hallway, down the steps, and out the cat flap. By the time I open the downstairs door he's halfway up our short street, pausing to see whether I'm following. He sees me and shoots up and across into the woods.

The impertinent beast! How had he known I wasn't at my desk that looks out on the courtyard? Grrrrr…

Upstairs, Ariel's asleep and Agrippa comes out from beneath the guest bed, apparently relieved that I've finally frightened Sylvester away. Agrippa is at least two pounds heavier than the bully, by the way.

The next time Sylvester intrudes during the day, Charlie waits till the cat's upstairs, closes the downstairs door, and then chases him around the upstairs a few times before booting him out the front door with the soft end of a broom—very gently, we can't bear to harm cats.

"That'll dissuade him," said Charlie. "Now he knows we can trap him."

For several mornings the cat bowls aren't licked clean and neither of us encounters Sylvester upstairs.

Then one night I wake at 1:30 am and go out into the living room to read. Puck sits on my lap keeping me warm, and just as I'm thinking I'm nicely sleepy he leaps down and starts growling in the direction of the front door. Adrenaline rushes through my body as I tiptoe out into the entryway. The carport light's on— someone's tripped the motion detectors. But Puck's not looking out there, he's watching the landing on the stairs. His growl grows louder as a black and white head appears.

"Sylvester!" I shout and give chase.

Once again, he's out the cat flap before I can catch him.

Charlie's waiting at the top of the steps when I return. "I'll sleep downstairs the rest of the night," he mumbles.

I turn off the alarm and open the front door for Agrippa—he's the one who turned on the carport light.

And up the stairs bounds Ariel, singing her greeting.

"I don't know," Charlie says, "maybe Ariel the party girl invites him in for a good feed."

The next night we sleep on the sofa bed in the media room armed with flashlight, blanket and heavy gardening gloves (picking up an angry cat, you see). Puck takes up a position at the foot of the bed, watching the flap. Agrippa takes up position out in the courtyard. Ariel comes in and out, in and out, but finally settles down between us and we fall asleep. About 2:30 am Puck begins to growl. Growl isn't an accurate description of the noise he makes, which begins as a high, eerie shriek and then drops to a low guttural. I grab the blanket as the black and white head pokes through the double flap, but Agrippa's now right behind Sylvester out in the courtyard and lets out a shriek. Sylvester's out and up the street before we even figure out who's going to turn on the flashlight when I'm holding a blanket and Charlie's wearing gardening gloves

We decide hey, it's winter, Ariel and the others shouldn't be out at night in the cold, we'll just lock the cat flap after dinner.

Three months later, as the evenings get longer, Ariel's getting wise and not coming in for dinner until after we've gone to bed. But three months—surely Sylvester has forgotten and we can leave the flap open at night?

Hah. Agrippa begins hiding again, and the bowls are licked clean in the mornings. Charlie camps out downstairs and one night

Sylvester even manages to sneak past him! I find him up in the kitchen. Was there ever such a bold cat??? We develop theories about his owner—someone who gets home at 2:30 am and lets the cat out for the night—perhaps a chef. A bartender.

I have a brilliant idea. Cats dislike water. If I set the sprinklers closest to the house to come on at 2:20 am for 10 minutes, Sylvester might give the courtyard a go. And just to cinch it, I'll set the outer sprinklers for 2:30 am. If he waits till the sprinklers close to the house stop and then slips beneath the fence into the courtyard, the outer sprinklers will trap him in the sogginess for 10 minutes. One experience with that and he'll be discouraged all right. But just to be sure, we keep them set through the spring. A rainy spring. The courtyard gets soggier and soggier, the moss actually looks as if it needs mowing, and the mushrooms—unbelievable. So after several months of wee hours watering we decide to see whether Sylvester has given us up.

Hah!

Fortunately it's been a dry summer. But when we shut down the sprinkler system for the winter, we'll lock the cat flap at night. And then I'm going door to door to find out just what Sylvester's owner does at 2:30 am.

Photo Courtesy of Steven Miller.

Keri Healey is a playwright, director, and actor living in Seattle. Her work includes the plays *Don't You Dare Love Me*, *One Twelve*, *Cherry Cherry Lemon*, *Penetralia*, and *The IKEA Cycle: Tiny Domestic Dramas* (co-written with Bret Fetzer). Her plays have been performed in Seattle, Austin, Dallas, Minneapolis, Vail, Australia, England, Canada, and Singapore. Keri is also the author of a collection of short stories entitled *Jealous of Boys*. In 2004, she was chosen by Seattle Dramatists as one of its five inaugural Principal Playwrights. In 2005, she was selected by *The Stranger* as "One to Watch" in their annual Genius Awards issue.

Keri read her story, *On the Coffee Table*, at the 2008 event themed "Night Hawk."

ON THE COFFEE TABLE

There was one thing that George McKeon was one hundred percent right about and that was this: on six out of seven days a week, no one in the world gave a damn about him. Not his father, who was usually working two shifts and too tired even to cook spaghetti when he got home; and not his mother since she was long gone. His brother Gary was in the county lockup for the time being for selling marijuana in the park, but even before he got arrested, he didn't give a damn about George. Gary would steal George's baseball cards to sell at the Sunday swap meet over behind St. Thomas Church.

"I'm a businessman, Georgie," he would say when George found his stacks of cards had been pilfered. "These aren't doing anyone any good just sitting up here in your room."

No one else cared about George McKeon either. Not Mr. and Mrs. Sterenberg who lived next door. Not the construction workers who poured foundations at the Windsor Glen housing development nearby, where George would wander after dark by himself, sometimes leaving handprints on the drying concrete. Not the guy who worked Saturdays at the deli, who looked like the guy on "Welcome Back, Kotter," not John Travolta but the other one with the curly hair. That guy at the deli always suspected George was shoplifting when he came in, not because he was, but just because. He never thought about George, though, outside of his Saturday shift, after work when he would meet up with Angela Mucci at Frank's for a slice and a soda. Outta sight, outta mind. These damn kids. That's just the way it was in their neighborhood.

There was a teacher, though, Miss DeFeo, who seemed to care about George McKeon. Maybe not every week, but still. Miss DeFeo would occasionally call George back into her classroom after the bell rang, just call after him from her desk as he shuffled out of her room, four or five books clutched clumsily under his arm. She would ask him something and he would mumble something back or shake his head. And then maybe she would ask him something else, or even offer a suggestion, perhaps guessing at a book that he might like to read, basically taking just a few minutes of his time now and then — nothing more — to let him know he was actual and alive and noticed.

At least, that's what it looked like from my locker.

I'd known George for years, ever since we moved to Newburgh from Long Island when I was seven. He lived down the street from us. He would sometimes come over to play in my backyard, sometimes when my dad would set up the pool in the summer for all the neighbor kids to play in. He wasn't an official friend, though, until fifth grade. When I was eleven years old, George and I tied for first place at Noble Hill K though eight's annual art fair and, after that, we were forever linked in the minds of faculty and community. This was a net gain for neither of us for even though I wasn't stuck with George's fifth grade enemies or his general reputation for creepiness, I didn't have friends of any real stature to help dilute that creepiness. Susan Katz, the better dressed of my two best friends, warned me that George's family was part of a secret cult.

"It's common knowledge," she told me. "They eat ground dog."

George came to my twelfth and thirteenth birthday parties. Susan Katz, who obviously hated George but for no clear reason other than his general creepiness and the rumors about the dog meat, let this fact slide the first year, but protested loudly the second time it happened.

"I thought this was supposed to be an ALL GIRLS slumber party!"

"It is," I told her. "He has to leave at ten."

"That's just stupid. Who ever heard of an all girls slumber party with a BOY? Especially an ugly one."

"He's not a boy if he's gay," volunteered Donna Jo Incalcaterra, the more rational and sophisticated of my two best friends. "It's all right if he stays if he's gay because then it doesn't matter if he sleeps in the same room with us."

The truth is, I didn't know if George was gay or not. Not at thirteen when Andy Gibb and staying up all night were the two greatest things I could ask for and not at fifteen when George and I got detention together and Susan Katz stopped talking to me. George WAS the first person to ever try to explain to me what gay meant, though — in third grade, in the library, when he asked me if I knew what a hobo was.

"Isn't it someone who rides on trains?" I answered, still asking.

George corrected me.

"No, it's two guys who marry each other."

There's a reason why I'm thinking about George McKeon today — twenty five years after high school, after I left Newburgh, never to look back, only managing to send Christmas cards each year and make the occasional Mother's Day call. There's a reason, and I will get to that. Just know that it starts in my living room. I mean, in my parents' living room. Nineteen eighty.

There is a book. My father's favorite book. It's been around forever in our living room, so long I hardly noticed it anymore although at one point in our lives, much earlier, before so much had happened, it used to be the reason I would sit on my father's lap for hours, staring at the pages as he turned them slowly. A big, gigantic book with shiny, thick pages. And on the cover, a reproduction of a painting. A quiet diner, late at night. The place is empty, just three people sitting on stools and one man behind the counter, reaching under it to put something away or maybe wipe something up. He's working and the customers are sitting there...waiting. No one's on the street outside the diner. No one's rushing around. It's still and it's quiet. Everyone else must be in bed, already asleep.

I come home after school one day — this is my sophomore year, nineteen eighty. When I enter my bedroom, my mother is sitting on my bed, the big, gigantic book in her lap, its spine opened.

"Why would you do this?" she asks me.

"Do what?"

"You know what I mean."

"No. I don't," I say.

"Why would you deface your father's property like this?"

"I didn't deface anything," I tell her.

"Don't lie to me."

"I'm not lying."

"You never used to lie to me."

"I swear I'm NOT LYING. I don't even know what you're talking about."

We are at an impasse, my mother and me. It's been coming for a few years, but here is it. We don't have anything huge to fight over anymore. All the huge stuff has already happened. Now, we pick on these tiny things, these superfluous little assaults.

"THIS is what I'm talking about," my mother says and she shoves the big, gigantic book toward me. "THIS. Here."

I couldn't see what she was referring to. All I saw were some sketches on a page, a bunch of text, someone trying to explain what the sketches meant or how and when they were drawn.

"LOOK." And her finger traces over the shorn edge of a page that is now missing from the book. A page that has been cut out carefully with a sharp knife. Traces slowly along the inside of the book's spine, from one end to the other, her eyes locked on me as I watch the accusing finger move.

"I didn't do that," I tell her.

"Then who did?"

"Why is it always me, huh?"

"Then tell me who did it," she orders me.

"I said I didn't do it, so I didn't do it. Why do you always blame ME for everything?"

And I knew she wouldn't dare to answer this one. My mother wouldn't dare to say out loud that I was the only child she had left to blame.

"Huh? Tell me. Why me?"

My mother gets up off my bed, book still in her hands, and charges into the living room. I yell after her.

"And what's the big deal anyway? What's the big deal about one lousy page? There are still about three hundred other stupid pages left in the book."

"You don't understand anything about having anything nice. You just don't care."

"I care."

"This is a coffee table book. It's not something you cut out like a magazine for your little art projects."

(As if she knew anything about my art projects.)

"A coffee table book is something someone gives you. It's not careless. It's not an afterthought. It's something someone has selected carefully because they know you will want to look at it every day, you will find joy inside it. It will be something that you find special and that you remember for the rest of your life."

"Well, maybe you shouldn't care so much about THINGS," I mumble, not really trying to keep it under my breath.

"What did you just say to me?" she asks.

"We don't even have a stupid coffee table. So why the HELL would we need a COFFEE TABLE BOOK?"

In the nearly thirty years that have passed since that afternoon, I spent most days believing my situation to be the exact opposite of George's. I believed that on six out of seven days a week, not only did someone in the world give a damn about me, but that everyone in the world gave a damn about me. Everyone was watching over me. Everyone, hovering, never leaving me alone. Anticipating my trips and falls, preventing anything potentially painful, unsafe, or even remotely unpredictable from happening to me. Because, this is what happens when your sister dies in a car wreck.

But I was wrong. When parents lose a child, it is assumed — maybe even actually felt in the bones and skin for a time — that all their love and attention will spill down onto the surviving sibling, surrounding and protecting the remainder child, drowning her. I've come to understand, however, that the opposite is true. When parents lose a child, all their love and attention rises upward, uncertain of where to go, what to latch onto, rises up as if reaching toward the tops of mountains, their grief acting as a particle accelerator, their love and attention spinning furiously and, finally, smashing like atoms and spraying outward. One of these parents will spend her nights pulling the dead child's hair from old brushes, leaving just enough so that there's more to pull tomorrow night. The other parent will retreat into the third person storytelling of the arts, of books, of symphonies that place his grief in an anonymous, everyman context, so that he doesn't have to see his name spelled out within its definition. My parents dissolved and floated away before I reached my sixteenth birthday. They weren't visible to me anymore and I became part of the general landscape to them, just as George did to his family. We co-existed harmoniously but learned to accurately estimate the distance between each other so as not to collide.

My seventeenth birthday was actually the last party I remember attending where I was the guest of honor. I had invited George but he told me he couldn't make it because he was taking an extra shift. George worked Saturdays at the deli by that time, with the guy who looked like the guy from "Welcome Back, Kotter," only older. It wasn't much of a party. Donna Jo and her boyfriend came over, a few others from swing choir, but I left them all making out on the floor of our family room and I slipped out our back sliding door to walk over to George's house where he was home in his living room, watching TV.

"I knew you didn't have to work," I said to him. He shrugged.

"Wanna see something?" he asked. I nodded and he led the way upstairs to his bedroom, taking the stairs two steps at a time.

"Wait out here," he told me, and I stood there while he went back into his room and shut the door for a few minutes. I could hear him rushing around, moving things, clicking switches, rustling sheets of paper. When he came back out he told me to close my eyes before he pulled my arm, leading me into his room and onto a bean bag chair on the floor.

When I opened my eyes a minute later at his command, I saw a gallery of at least a hundred reprints of paintings, some of which I recognized from our field trips to the museums in the city, some of which I studied in class. A stunning cacophony of color, a mixture of aggressive and subtle brush strokes, photographs so sharp you could almost feel your finger pressing into the wet globs of paint soaking into the canvas. George had taken at least a hundred cheap flashlights and wrapped wire around them, attaching them to a master wire that he ran across each wall. He did this row after row, inventing his own homemade track lighting system, a hundred spectacular dots sprayed against the wall. I'd never seen anything quite as beautiful, not even in the real museums themselves.

"Can you guess which one's my favorite?" he asked me.

I didn't have to. My eye went straight to it. I knew that painting. I have known it since I could walk. A quiet diner, late at night. The place is empty, just three people sitting on stools and one man behind the counter, reaching under it to put something away or maybe wipe something up. Page one-fifty-seven of my father's coffee table book.

"It's Edward Hopper," George told me.

"Yeah," I said. "I know. The king of light and loneliness."

But George told me that he didn't see Hopper as lonely at all. "He loves windows and rooftops," George said, "and hotel rooms and theater lobbies. That's not lonely, that's alive. He puts coffee cups on tables and makes women read books on trains. I want to live where he lives someday."

There's a reason why I'm thinking about George McKeon today. And that is this: tonight I am getting on a plane headed toward Newburgh. My mother died this week. I will attend the funeral that Mrs. McCarville from across the street helped to arrange and I will assist my father in cleaning out Mom's belongings. He's thinking there might be some clothes or jewelry that I might want to keep.

The Hopper picture arrived in my mail today. A little crumpled and folded over and over again to fit into the envelope. Overnighted from Newburgh. From Philo Street. Signed, George McKeon.

I'm going home.

Photo Copyright © Deb Ching.

Brenda Peterson is the author of 16 books, including the classic *Living by Water: True Stories of Nature and Spirit, Duck and Cover*, a *New York Times* "Notable Book of the Year" and the recent memoir, *I Want To Be Left Behind: Finding Rapture Here on Earth*, from which this story is adapted. This book was selected by independent booksellers nationwide as a "Top Pick." For more on Brenda and her work please visit www.IWantToBeLeftBehind.com.

Brenda read at the 2004 Bedtime Stories event themed "Dreamland."

BEAUTIFICATION

Many summers my parents left us with my grandfather and Jessie, his second wife. We grandchildren all adored Jessie because when she was not in the Ozarkian farm kitchen fixing her famous hush puppies, butter beans, and a sinfully delicious blueberry cobbler, she was in town at her garage beauty studio, *Chez Jessie.* Most thrilling of all, she also moonlighted as a hairstylist in the small-town morgue, offering the residents her "beautification," as she called it.

The "ladies" in Jessie's hair salon took great comfort in knowing that Jessie would dramatically sculpt their hair for the biggest dress formal of their lives—their funerals. I'd heard some church folk joke that Southern Baptist weddings seemed as dutiful as funerals and Baptist funerals were the real weddings. After all, what woman wouldn't want to be a Bride of Christ with no housework or endless chores, lazing about in the Father's many mansions? For their posthumous debut Jessie promised her clients a perm that was a "primp for eternity." Her clients would go to their glory and meet their Maker in style. Some of them looked even more radiant and well-dressed dead than alive, since no expense was spared at Southern Baptist funerals and people saved up over decades for this big show—when they would receive their heavenly reward. Jessie often adorned her late ladies with shiny barrettes and rhinestone baubles as symbolic of the "stars in their crowns."

I always wondered what souls actually did in heaven, besides sing and praise God. I imagined that maybe everyone was still in school, an eternal afterlife of study with recess anytime we wanted to stretch our wings.

Once in fourth grade, I had a vivid dream. In my little wooden desk with the folding top carved in hieroglyphics, I saw that I was surrounded by others who all happened to be very studious snakes. Our teacher was a luminous King Cobra raised up in her full, hooded glory. But she did not strike; she swayed and danced. On the blackboard behind her were listed possible classes:

Understanding
Forgiveness
Helpfulness
Stillness
Mercy
Hopefulness
Loving Kindness

I decided on "Forgiveness" and "Loving Kindness" but was told, not unkindly by the teacher, that this was too heavy a class load for one life. I must choose. I looked down, disappointed in myself, and only then casually noticed that I too was a snake, but not poisonous. I was a little garter snake like the slippery ones that my father taught us not to kill because they were good for the garden. That significant sign helped me decide my course of study. I chose the "Loving Kindness" curriculum, also called "Compassion 101." My life's major choice seemed really to please the white cobra teacher because she hissed, "That is a most difficult class."

At that age, I knew nothing of Buddhism or any other religion that assumed reincarnation. It would not be until high school and world history that I would hear of other spiritual traditions and their beliefs in many lives. For now, all I knew was that my dreams were as real as daily life. My dreams were as much a home to me as a parallel universe. The Bible and its fantastic stories also seemed an alternate universe. Otherwise, how could someone living in northern Virginia in the early Sixties amid segregation riots and a suspiciously Catholic president also be living in her spiritual imagination in places like Canaan or Jerusalem or, better yet, the astonishing visions of Revelation? In that last book of the Bible, John's dreams of End Times were so full of magical animals, they rivaled any bestiary.

What many don't understand about the most fundamentalist Christians is that the feral quality of their imaginations is bred on a Bible that is not read as symbolic but as the absolute Word of God. Miracles, dreams, and the afterlife enliven a daily reality often prescribed and rigid. My parents are not extreme fundamentalists. As they've grown older, they have not followed their Southern Baptist Convention into its far-right rigidity. They now ascribe to themselves the term "socially conservative evangelicals." But they still firmly believe in a Rapture interpretation of End Times. They dream of another world nearby where God dwells and where they hope to be lifted up to meet Him midair. Meanwhile, they wait and dream.

God often talked to prophets like Daniel and directed their lives and an entire kingdom through dreams. But any magic in the real world, or especially in nature, is suspect—or worse, of the Devil. Didn't Satan often use animals, such as the serpent, to beguile us? Anyone paying too much attention to trees or animals might be accused of communing not with nature but with evil. As a dreamy child, often distracted by the radiant world outside the high church windows, I was often chided for not listening. It was not my intention to be disrespectful. I could listen as well as look.

In this context, my dream that I was studying in a seminary school for snakes was not all that strange. Revelations and End Times prophecies made my little dreams look tame. Nevertheless, I knew enough about the bad rep that snakes had gotten in the Bible never to tell the dream to anyone. I really liked snakes and was intrigued that the subtle serpent had once been a favorite angel. If snakes were good for our earthly gardens, why was the Satan serpent so bad for the Garden of Eden? Scientifically, this Bible story had never made much sense to me. I also liked trees so much that the Tree of Knowledge being off-limits always bothered me. And why, if Paradise was once here on earth, could we not rediscover it again, like a lost world, by becoming explorers as in *National Geographic*, my favorite magazine?

If I were ever going to confide some of my true beliefs or dreams, it would be to my step-mother, Jessie. She loved and gossiped with her huge garden like a family. In that rural backwoods she was what was called a "yarb doctor" who used plants and herbs for healing. With these herbs, her beauty parlor potions, and her quick wit, Jessie was more pagan than even she knew. But I didn't realize that; I only knew that my patriarch of a grandfather, who seemed the very fearful image of God the Father, was devoted to Jessie and so was I. Since I was still smarting from being bounced from Vacation Bible School this summer, I was looking for a role model upon whom to model my religious life. Jessie seemed a fine candidate. Jessie told me that God was in her garden and by tending her green world she was being a faithful servant. She didn't kill snakes either.

By planting God firmly in her garden, and so in this lush world, Jessie gave me a grounded sense of hope about being here. She was a good Christian, though not a fundamentalist. Even today, my step-grandmother will make a distinction that many of the faithful do: science should pay more attention to dreams, wonders, and miracles—for God is everywhere suffused in nature.

When science strips away the spiritual dimensions, even many moderate Christians, like Jessie, feel secular scientists are godless and perhaps not to be believed.

Jessie was stunningly beautiful. Black-blue hair curled in a French coif, perfect Modigliani face and olive skin with the brightest fuchsia lipstick in the county. Her elegance was the unspoken envy of many townswomen. To me, she was more enthralling than any movie star.

Jessie's birthday gift to me that summer was a permanent. While I sat in her beauty parlor chair, I asked her if she thought God had a wife or mother or daughter, since women seemed strangely absent in the Old and New Testaments.

"You're the scripture gal," Jessie teased me, just as she was teasing my thin hair into a storm of dark blond ringlets, held in a beehive by blue goo called Dippity-Do and a steady mist of hair spray so foul-smelling I had a choking fit. "Any mention of God's kinswomen in the Bible?"

"Not many," I admitted. "I've looked for them everywhere, but except for Eve and Ruth and Naomi, and maybe Deborah, the Jewish judge, and Mary Magdalene." I paused, and looked at her meaningfully in the mirror. "Of course, there *was* Jezebel."

I perked up at the sound of this forbidden woman's name.

"Now," Jessie laughed and slapped my knee, "I bet that gal was a lot of fun, don't you? Probably just having too good a time for her own good."

"Yes, ma'am!"

"Don't know if God is really a woman," Jessie concluded, appreciatively eyeing my new perm. "But I do believe he needs to find hisself a better half."

God the Father definitely needed the civilizing and kindly helpmate of a wife and mother, I agreed. Noah had one; so did Abraham, the patriarch who would obediently almost slay his own son; unforgiving Lot and long-suffering Job and, of course, Adam—the man my grandfather believed was "henpecked."

For all his bluster, we all knew that Grandfather was beholden to Jessie. He loved her desperately, still acting, even after decades together, like a suitor. Years younger than my grandfather, Jessie would sometimes cajole him as he lounged idly on the porch swing, "See that old thang? That *used* to be your grandfather!"

I wanted so much to be like Jessie that when she spun me around in her beauty parlor chair to look at my birthday coif in the mirror I did not gasp out loud. My crimped curls looked like Shirley Temple after the electric chair. Swallowing hard, I told Jessie this perm was just what I needed to start fifth grade. Secretly, I knew I would be relentlessly ridiculed.

Yet squinting through the haze of hair spray Jessie aimed at me, I had an epiphany: I believed Jessie would have made a very good wife of God. Or maybe just a misunderstood, high-spirited Jezebel. Yes, I decided, from then on my snake dream of Compassion 101 and my step-grandmother, Jessie, who "beautified" all things, would be my spiritual guides. ~

Photo Copyright © by Mary Randlett.

Charles Johnson read his story *Night Hawks* at the 2008 event themed "Night Hawk."

NIGHT HAWKS

"Your right is to action alone; never to its fruits
at any time. Never should the fruits of action be
your motive; never let there be attachment to
inaction in you."

Bhagavad Gita, Book II, sloka 47

Seven or sevenish

Playwright August Wilson and I always met at 7 PM at the
Broadway Bar and Grill, which was just a short walk from his
many-roomed home on Capitol Hill in Seattle. We looked for the
smoker's section at the rear of the restaurant in a spacious, dimly-
lit room with two televisions mounted on the peach-colored
walls. He would arrive as tidily dressed as ever, his demeanor
courtly and dignified, even gracious, with his salt-and-pepper
goatee neatly trimmed, and wearing a stylish, plaid cap on his
balding head. (He once told me, "I should just *stop* going to the
barber shop.") We were two old men with a combined 100-plus
years of American history on our heads, only three years apart
in age, and raised in the 1940s and '50s by proud, hard-working
parents. You might say that for fifteen years these eight to ten
hour dinner conversations at the Broadway were our version of a
boys' night out. It was a lively, laid-back place filled with young

people, straights and gays, students and Goths, and much nicer than the dangerous place we would end up in before this evening was over.

After a handshake and a hug, we would sit down, order organic Sumatra French Roast coffee and a big plate of chicken Nachos with black beans, olives and guacamole. Then we began the ritual that defined for me our friendship. We always tried to remember to bring some kind of gift for each other. It was a ritual of respect, generosity, and civility. The presents we gave each other were always art, or about art, and each represented our life-long passion for the creative process. Because he knew I was a cartoonist and illustrator, he would give me, say, the tape of a documentary showing Picasso at work, or *The Complete Cartoons of the New Yorker* and *The Complete Far Side* by Gary Larsen. I, in turn, would give him a limited-edition, facsimile reproduction of one of Jorge Luis Borges' short story manuscripts presented to me during a State Department-sponsored lecture tour in Spain, because Borges, Amiri Baraka, Romare Bearden and the blues, or the "Four B's" as August called them, were the major influences on his work.

Eight o' clock
Finally, after we'd examined and discussed our gifts, and the waiter, a thin girl, leggy and tattooed, with bright red hair and a nose-ring, returned to top off our coffee for the second time, we'd relax and let our hair down. This experience, we both knew, was extremely rare in the lonely, solitary lives of writers, especially those considered to be successful by the way the world judged things, so we sometimes looked at each other as if to say, "How did *you* happen?" This unstated question was filled with equal parts of curiosity and affection, partly because he and I belonged to an in-between, liminal generation that remembered segregation yet was also the fragile bridge to the post-civil rights period and

beyond; and partly because American culture had changed so much since we began writing in the 1960s, growing coarser, more vulgar and selfish year by year, distancing itself from the vision of our parents who were raised to value good manners, promise-keeping, personal sacrifice, loyalty to their own parents and kin, and a deep-rooted sense of decency. On the stage, his goal was to make audiences respect their hardscrabble lives and his own. This new era of Hip Hop, misogynistic gangsta rap, and profanity-laced ghetto-lit sometimes made our souls feel like they needed to take a shower. He told me often that if he ever met the Wayans Brothers, he planned on slapping both of them silly.

"You know what?" I could tell by the tilt of his head that he felt playful tonight. "When I was out of town for rehearsal these last few months, I'd leave my hotel room, walk over to the theater, and every day I'd see the same man panhandling on the street. He stopped me every day, and every time he had something new for me, so I had to give him some money. For example, one day he pointed down at my feet, and he said, 'I *know* where you got those good-lookin' shoes. I can *tell* you exactly where you got those fancy shoes.'"

The man August was describing could easily have been an antic character in one of his plays.

"You got 'em on your *feet*," he said. "But I know somethin' else, too. I know the day you were born. I can *tell* you the very day you were born, and I won't be wrong or off by more than three days."

August was born on April 27, 1945.

When he asked this fellow what day he was born, the man cackled and said *Wednesday*.

And so it went for fifteen years of *pas de deux*. Sometimes we'd lean into the table to hear each other better when our voices were blurred by the clatter and clang of dishes and swirl of laughter and conversation from other tables around us, talking about our hopes for our children, our wives, our agents and lawyers and business partners, the next story we planned to write for Humanities Washington's yearly Bedtime Stories fundraiser, a passage I translated for him that he liked from the *Bhagavad-Gita*, and our works-in-progress—*Gem of the Ocean* and *Radio Golf* for him, the novel *Dreamer* for me. But for the most part, and because I'm Buddhist, I did the lion's share of listening. Also because my middle-class life in the Chicago suburb of Evanston had not been half as hard as his in the Hill District of Pittsburgh. He wanted someone to listen as he spoke about his life, all the experiences and ideas not always in his plays but which were, in fact, the background for his ten-play cycle. Over fifteen years, I heard about his biological father Frederick Kittel, the German baker who was always absent from his life, and his step-father, an ex-convict who spent twenty-three years in prison for robbery and murder. He adopted his mother's maiden name, Wilson, in rejection of his German father; he began using his middle name, August, when a friend told him not to let anyone call him by the first name he used throughout childhood, which was Freddie. August told me that when he entered the newly-integrated public schools of Pittsburgh, he was attacked by a gang of other kids; the principal had to send him home in a taxi cab to protect him, but all he could do was ask over and over, *"Why?* Why are they trying to hurt *me?* What did *I* do?"* And I learned about why he dropped out of high school his freshman year when a black teacher accused him of plagiarizing a twenty-page term paper entitled "Napoleon's Will to Power" and refused to apologize.

Out of school at age sixteen, he worked at menial jobs. "I dropped out of high school, not life," he often said, and that was true: he may not have been a formally trained intellectual, but he was an organic one, who read shelf after shelf of books at his local library, and dreamed of becoming a writer. No, he was not in school, but he did have a reliable and constant teacher: suffering. "If you want to be a writer," a prostitute once told him, "then you better learn how to write about *me*." He did take her advice. He also joined the Army, and was doing quite well but, being a proud and hot-blooded young man, he left when he was told he was still too young to apply for officer's training school. There was a year in his life when he was a member of the Nation of Islam, an organization he joined because he hoped to win back the love of his Muslim wife after she unexpectedly left him, taking their daughter and stripping their home clean of every stick of furniture. Entering those barren rooms, said August, was so devastating and heart-breaking that this shock of emptiness washed the strength from his limbs. How many times had his heart been broken? He could not remember the countless disappointments. Like so many writers and artists I've known, his art was anchored in lacerations and a lattice-work of scar-tissue. All that raw pain, poverty and disappointment, denial and disrespect—as when critic Robert Brustein said he had "an excellent mind for the twelfth century"—all *this* he alchemized into plays that, before his death in 2005, earned him two Pulitzer Prizes, eight New York Drama Critic Circle Awards, a Tony Award, an Olivier Award, a National Humanities Medal presented by Bill Clinton, a Broadway theater renamed in his honor, and twenty-eight honorary degrees.

Yet the public could only know the media-created surface, not the subterranean depths, of any artist. Every time you sat down to create something your soul was at stake. Every page—indeed, every paragraph—had been a risk. Every sentence had been a prayer. So when speaking of those honorary degrees, August told me that he recently came across one of them in his attic and suddenly burst into tears because he couldn't for the life of him remember this particular award that was so dear bought with his own emotional blood. What no one knew of, or could know, was that after every one his ten plays opened, he fell into a period of severe depression that always lasted for two solid weeks.

He talked freely because he knew I understood these things, how despite the strong black male personas our past pain made us present to the world, we were far more sensitive than we could ever dare show (and *had* to be sensitive and vulnerable in order to create), with the external world being no more than raw material for our imaginations, and that meant we were eccentric: he didn't drive, or do e-mail, or exercise, and if someone walking a dog came his way on the sidewalk, he would step into the street because dogs frightened him, why I can't say. More than once he shared with me his fantasy of finishing his ten plays and telling the world he was retiring. Then, when the reporters went away, the phone stopped ringing, and he vanished from public view, August planned on sitting on his Capitol Hill porch reading piles of books he never had the time to get to, playing with his young daughter, and writing without interruption or distraction for a decade. When that ten years ended, he said, he planned to emerge from seclusion like Eugene O'Neill after *his* decade away from the spotlight, and with plays that would be as powerful and enduring as *The Iceman Cometh, Long Day's Journey Into Night*, and *A Moon for the Misbegotten*. He also hoped one day to write a novel.

Those nights at the Broadway Bar and Grill, he needed to talk about things like this. And sometimes he expressed a fear that shook me to my very foundations.

Midnight

At some point during our conversations his thoughts always turned to the ambiguous state of black America. Like the narrator of Charles Dickens' *A Tale of Two Cities*, you could say for black America that "It was the best of times, it was the worst of times." August and I were doing well, he said, but he couldn't forget the fact that Broadway theater tickets were expensive and twenty-five percent of black people lived in poverty, and therefore never saw his plays. He said there were too many black babies born out of wedlock and without fathers in their homes. Too many young black men were in prison, or the victims of murder. Too many were living with the HIV virus. It was as if forty years after the end of the Jim Crow era, black America was falling apart.

"So let me ask you a question," he said. We'd long ago finished our entrées (the Dungeness Crab sandwich for me, the Grilled Cedar Plank Salmon for him) and had lost count of how many times the waiter had filled our coffee cups. The last four hours had passed as if they were only fifteen minutes. Only a sprinkling of people remained in the rear of the Broadway Bar and Grill, which was less noisy now so his voice was clear against the background of music drifting from the front room. "Do you think any of it matters?"

"What?"

"Everything we've done." His eyes narrowed a little and smoke spiraled up his wrist from his cigarette. "Nothing we've done changes or improves the situation of black people. We're still powerless and disrespected every day—by everyone and ourselves. People still think black men are violent and lazy and stupid. They see you and me as the exceptions, not the rule."

"You don't see any real changes since the sixties?"

"No," he said, "Not really."

For a moment I didn't know what to say. I knew he meant all this. You could see it in his plays, that sense of despair, futility and stasis. If he was right, then I wondered, What *good* was art? And his words took the philosopher in me to an even deeper dread. If you paused for just a moment and pulled back from our minuscule dust mote of a planet in one of a hundred billion galaxies pinwheeling across a 13 billion-year-old universe that one day would experience proton death, then it was certain all that men and women had ever done would one day be as if it never was. I wondered: Had we then wasted our lives? Was man, as Sartre put it in *Being and Nothingness*, "a useless passion"?

Two o'clock.
I was about to press him on this point about the social impotence of art and, by virtue of that, ourselves, but now our waiter was standing beside us.

"I'm sorry, but you guys are going to have to go. We need to close."

We paid our bill, left a generous tip, and stepped outside to the empty street, talking on the wide strip of cement for another hour. Both of us realized that this business of whether art mattered beyond the easily forgotten awards and evanescent applause was an issue that had re-energized us—or maybe it was the coffee we'd been drinking for the last seven hours. Also, we both knew it was still too early to go home to our wives. Accordingly, August suggested we find a twenty-four-hour place so we could keep on talking. The only restaurant open was a nearby International House of Pancakes. We climbed into my Jeep Wrangler, and drove south on East Broadway to Madison Street, where I hung a left and after one block down-shifted into the helter skelter of a parking lot. Something was wrong here. There was a blue-and-white police car outside I-hop and a cop was talking to one of the employees wearing a gray, short-sleeved shirt and a blue apron. As nearly as I could tell, something had happened just before we arrived, perhaps a robbery, but we didn't know for sure. Confused but not ready to give up on the night, we stepped around the police car and went through the double doors inside.

Three o'clock

The dining area was a brightly-lit rectangle with two ceiling fans turning slowly and booths arranged along the walls and down the middle. Unlike the Broadway, the customers in I-hop at this hour were nighthawks, the people who slept all day and only ventured out after dark: a group that may have included the occasional prostitute, gang-banger, pimp, or drug dealer. No one seemed to recognize either of us as famous writers. A fidgety waiter seated us in a booth behind the cash register. I saw the police car pull away. Inside, the air felt tense and fibrous. The other patrons were poker-faced and skittish, speaking in whispers, watching for something, their eyes occasionally flashing with fear. August noticed this, too, but he said nothing. He was more at home in this setting than I was. It was a replay of Pittsburgh's Hill District. He knew what to expect. I didn't. When the waiter brought us two cups of flat, brackish coffee, we tried to resume our conversation, but try as I might, I couldn't concentrate on his words. And what happened next I had not expected. The front doors opened, and two young men wearing lots of bling—the one in front compact in build, the one behind him tall and thin like Snoop Dog—walked straight past a waiter who tried to seat them, and headed toward a table in the back where two women sat with a chuffy-cheeked young man whose complexion was pitted and pock-marked. The first man, handsome and clean-timbered, with the plucky confidence of the actor Ice Cube, began singing at the man who was seated. But wait. It wasn't singing. It was rap. A kind of rhymed challenge. I couldn't make out the words. Being an old gaffer, I could *never* keep up with the japper of fast-talking rappers, but everyone in I-hop sat listening, frozen in their seats and afraid of this situation. Then he and his companion laughed and walked back to the lobby. A moment later, the man with bad skin stood up, clenching and unclenching his fists, and he walked with long strides to the lobby, too. I could tell they were talking. A few seconds passed. Then all at once I heard a tumult, a crash, a sound of shattering glass. I half stood on the red seat beneath me to see better. The first two men sailed like furies into the third, smashing wooden high chairs over his head. He jack-knifed at the waist and I heard a *flump* as he hit the floor. The other two stomped his fingers and kicked his face to a pulp, breaking bone and cartilage. Then they fled. Their victim staggered weakly to his feet, his breath tearing in and out of his chest, blood gushing from his lips. Then he, too, reeled out into the night.

The fight was over in ten seconds. All that time I'd been holding my breath. Finally, I faced round to August. But he was gone. Not too surprisingly, I picked him out in a crowd of customers who had wisely scrambled toward the exit at the back of the room. The moment the fight started, his old Pittsburgh instincts had kicked in, telling him to duck for cover in case someone started shooting.

Four o'clock

It took the police only a few minutes to return to I-hop. The restaurant's manager apologized to the patrons for the incident, which surely would be reported in the next day's *Seattle Times* and seen as just more bad PR for black people. The manager said we didn't have to pay for anything we ordered. We felt shaken by what we'd seen. Forty years earlier, we could have been those young men destroying each other. I looked at him; he looked at me, and perhaps we both thought at the same time, *How did you happen?*

It went without saying that we figured it was finally time to go home to our wives and children.

We stepped carefully around pools of blood, broken glass, and splinters of wood at the entrance, and returned to my Jeep in the early morning light, the air full of moisture. I said little. A strong rain wind slammed into the Jeep as I drove him home, making me hunch over the steering wheel. Finally, August broke the silence. He said, "People always ask me why black folks don't go to the theater. I try to tell them we've got *enough* ritual and drama in our lives already."

I stopped my Jeep in front of his house. We shook hands, and promised to get together again soon. Since his death, I often replay in my mind the image of America's most celebrated black playwright slowly climbing the steps to his front door; and at last I understood in what way decades devoted unselfishly day and night to art really mattered. The love of beauty had been our life-long refuge as black men, a raft that carried us both safely for sixty years across a turbulent sea of violence, suffering and grief to a far shore we'd never dreamed possible in our youth, one free of fear, and when his journey was over laid him gently, peacefully to eternal rest.

ACKNOWLEDGEMENTS

2010 Humanities Washington Board of Trustees
Your enthusiasm for this project has been immeasurable—thank you!

Lucia Huntington & Karen Munro (Co-Chairs)

John Baule
Diane Douglas
A.J. Epstein
David Freece
Ann Golden
Denise Harnly
Dan Lamberton
Susannah Malarkey
Ed Marquand
Sue McNab

Kris Molesworth
Bridget Piper
John Purdy
John Roth
Carli Schiffner
Dale Smith
Ricardo Valdez
Meredith Wagner
Cynthia Wells
Jan Walsh

2010 Humanities Washington Staff
. . . whose work furthers the impact of the humanities every day.

Julie Ziegler, Executive Director
Eric Sanders, Director of Finance
Ellen Terry, Director of Programs
Chris Thompson, Communications and Development Manager
Liv Woodstrom, Program Manager
Kari Dasher, Program Associate

Bedtime Stories Volunteers and Former Staff (1999-2009)

Bedtime Stories grew and flourished because of the work of a wonderful group of volunteers and the dedication of several former Humanities Washington staff members.. To you we owe our deepest gratitude!

Marna Abrams
Kathleen Alcalá
Kenny Alhadeff
Marleen Alhadeff
Steven Barnes
Lydia Bassett
John Baule
Greg Bear
Joanne Gordon Berk
Peter Blomquist
Margaret Ann Bollmeier
Rebecca Brown
Marité Butners
Deb Caletti
Ron Carlson
Patti Carter
Paul Chiocco
Lindsay Clothier
Chris Cooper
Elizabeth Crane
Gemma Valdez Daggatt
Mary Daheim
Mary Kay Davis
Karen Deitrick
Willy Delius
Tiffany Diamond
Barbara Dolby
Jane Dudley

Tananarive Due
Ruth Eller
Jack Faris
Ellen Ferguson
Roger Fernandes
Karen Fisher
Amanda Floan
Becky Fotheringham
Tess Gallagher
Nora Gallaher
Jean Gardner
Tod Goldberg
Sam Green
Bill Grinstein
David Guterson
Mary Guterson
Lynn Grant
Kim Hamilton
Jana Harris
Melissa Haumerson
Keri Healey
Teri Hein
Maureen Herward
Donald J. Horowitz
Linda Jaech
Margot Kahn
Laura Kalpakian
Bharti Kirchner

Martha Kongsgaard
Dan Lamberton
Kevin Laverty
Ted Lord
Susannah Malarkey
Louise Marley
Clark McCann
Pamela McClaran
Herman McKinney
Kris Molesworth
Colette Ogle
Therese Ogle
Dan Orozco
Nancy Pearl
Laura Penn
Brenda Peterson
Myra Platt
Stacey Plum
Karen Porterfield
Sherry Prowda
Reginald Andre Jackson
Charles Johnson
Margit Rankin
Jane Reich

Kathy Renner
Candace Robb
Tom Robbins
Catherine Rudolph
Judy Runstadt
Carlo Scandiuzzi
Lalie Scandiuzzi
Patrick Sexton
David Shields
David Skinner
Dale Smith
Carol Stromberg
Indu Sundaresan
Deborah Swets
Mayumi Tsutakawa
Jess Walter
Cynthia Wells
James Wilcox
Colleen Willoughby
August Wilson
Shawn Wong
Sarah Woods
Kathleen Woodward
Ann P. Wyckoff

CreateSpace.com

And finally, many thanks to the team at CreateSpace.com who expertly guided us through the publication of our first book and to whom we are indebted for their assistance in making these stories and essays available to a wider audience.

Made in the USA
Charleston, SC
21 November 2010